Flora
An Innocent Child?

A G Nuttall

First published by A G Nuttall 2025

This novel is entirely a work of fiction. The names, characters and incidents portrayed in it are the work of the author's imagination. Any resemblance to actual persons, living or dead, events or locales is entirely coincidental.

First edition 2025

978-1-0686691-7-0 (paperback)

angiebooks.com

I dedicate this book to my sister-in-law, Kirsty Russell.

CONTENTS

"... whoever does not receive the Kingdom of God as a little child will never enter it."
Luke 18:15-17.

A baby's cry pierced the silence. The sound of innocence entering the world, vulnerable and alone. Thrust into daylight, floundering in the openness of its surroundings, beginning a journey beyond the confines of its foetal home.

It longed for the voice that had spoken comfort, hummed and sang throughout life in the womb. It was fragile, totally dependent on the mother who had borne it.

The mother, a fifteen-year-old schoolgirl who had shamed her family with the betrayal of pregnancy, would be denied that role. The Sisters of St. Catharine's Convent would oversee her care.

The nuns were strict, sometimes cruel. They made no excuse for their odious feeling towards the unmarried mothers. Seeing them merely as sinners, aberrations before God's eyes.

When labour started, they offered no comfort, no matter the hours before the child appeared.

The baby was not excused from the sins of the mother, labelled bastard, unwanted, unloved, and ungodly. The child was tarnished from the moment it entered the world.

The nuns would nurture and raise the child in the eyes of God. Perhaps one day a suitable family would be found, but not before it had repented its sins.

Suddenly, that familiar voice cried out, "Flora…"

That was the last time she would hear her mother's voice, wailing in the distance, as Flora was ripped from her chest and hurried away.

Whatever the young mother's protestations, they made no difference to the fate of the child. The nuns ignored her tears and stitched cruelly between her legs. They offered her no sympathy, no pain relief. Their belief that the suffering she endured would act as a reminder the next time she chose to give herself so freely to a man.

They knew nothing of the child's conception, nor did they want to. They shied away from the girl's protestations, her cries of deceit. The horror of an unwanted pregnancy, the non-consensual violation she had suffered. The nuns heard only what they wanted to hear. They had already branded her with the same mark as the other mothers who visited them. One glance at her dyed hair and nail varnish had sealed her fate.

The girl's father was vicar of the local parish. A staunch believer and a proud Christian man who lived by the word of God. He could not allow his eldest daughter to tarnish that reputation, to flaunt her pregnancy to the God-fearing folk of the village. She had betrayed him, betrayed God, and betrayed herself.

He ordered that she leave at once before the evidence of her sin grew noticeable. One hundred miles away from everything and everyone that she knew. A place for mother and baby hidden behind the height of stone walls, where no one knew her.

I

"This is the child," declared Sister Ophelia, gently pulling Flora into view.

It was a process that had happened many times already in her short life. The meeting, the demanding questions, the distasteful expressions and the shake of the head. There was never a second visit.

"Age?" demanded the sour faced woman.

"Six," replied the nun.

"Small for her age," added the man, eyeing the child with a grimace.

"She's petite in stature, though her strength lies within," added the nun.

"You mean wilful," snorted the woman circling Flora.

"It's only to be expected in a child born of sin, but nothing that the pain of a belt buckle won't resolve," declared the man.

The couple turned their faces from view and muttered. It took under a minute for them to dismiss Flora and give their decision with a shake of the head.

"Very well!" remarked Sister Ophelia with a deep sigh. "Back to the kitchen, child," she soothed, ushering the couple to the door.

The children of St. Catharines Convent were paraded like zoo animals almost daily. Visitors would observe them, even touch them, dismiss them, and watch as they were herded away.

The odd child might be lucky enough to find a home from that process, though whether luck was the accurate description was debatable. Most were returned within a couple of weeks. Some were tortured, worked until the skin hung from their emaciated bones or died at the hands of their newfound family.

Children of the sinful were not to be loved and nurtured in the bosom of a caring home, but made to pay for the shame of their very existence. Hard work, regular beatings and stringency were all they deserved.

The belief was archaic, mistreat the child and you'll get more out of it. If only they would realise that the exact opposite was true, but people were too single-minded for change.

"Well?" demanded the Mother Superior of Sister Ophelia as they met in the hallway.

"I'm afraid not," shrugged the nun.

"You told them about her 'ability'?" queried Mother Superior sharply.

"Of course not," confirmed the nun, shaking her head.

"It's hard enough to gather interested couples for the other children," sighed the disgruntled Mother, "I fear Flora may never leave us."

"I'm sure God has a plan for her," proffered the nun tentatively.

"What's God got to do with it?" snapped the Mother Superior. "God plays no part in that child's life. She carries the mark of the Devil, and you'd do well to remember that."

The Mother Superior turned on her heels and left Sister Ophelia contemplating her words.

The ability of which the Reverend Mother spoke was as yet ill defined. Deemed to be the mark of the Devil by the order of nuns, even though the child showed no malicious or evil intent.

To the outside world, she was a small girl with golden curls, steel-blue eyes and a radiating smile, but Flora was much more than that.

She was capable of many things, mostly unexplained, and that was where the controversy lay.

Flora possessed an innate sixth sense. She knew how people were feeling just by looking at them as though she could read their thoughts. She knew what they were going to say before they spoke and for those reasons she upset the equilibrium of the Convent and disturbed the nuns.

In the kitchen, Flora had found space at the table and was busy peeling potatoes, one of her many chores throughout the day.

Sister Ophelia afforded her a smile. She differed from the other nuns. Perhaps life at the Convent had not yet withered her humanity. She was young and pretty, caring and kind. She held a place in her heart for Flora that she could never reveal.

"What are you smiling at, child?" growled Sister Regina.

The elderly nun who ran the kitchen was fierce, grotesque looking and emotionless. Age had weathered her already unfortunate features, leaving her with a horrifying profile. The children feared her face more than her cruelty.

Flora didn't reply.

"Are you deaf as well as stupid?" hissed the nun, grabbing Flora by the neck of her cotton apron.

"I'm sure she didn't hear you," interrupted Sister Ophelia softly.

"Didn't hear? Chose not to more like!" growled the nun, as she pulled Flora from her seat and threw her to the floor.

Flora said nothing. Her wide blue eyes gazed upon the face of Sister Regina as the old nun raised a hand to beat her, but the nun couldn't bring herself to chastise the child and lowered her hand with frustration. She walked away, to the amazement of everyone else in the kitchen, including Sister Ophelia.

Whatever the old nun had witnessed in Flora's eyes that day had unsettled her.

II

There was noise in the corridor outside Flora's dormitory. The sound of heels hitting the wooden floor woke her and several of the other girls.

Agnes, whose bed sat closest to the door, peeped through the keyhole as the rustle of black habits hurried by.

"Something's going on," she whispered. "It must be something serious for the nuns to be out of bed during the night."

The girls of the dormitory huddled together.

"Flora, you're freezing," declared Daphne, wrapping the child's tiny body in the thinness of her own blanket.

"Thank you," muttered Flora, welcoming the warmth of Daphne's generosity.

"Have you been out of bed again?" scolded Agnes.

Flora shook her head.

"Then why are you so cold?"

"I gave my blanket to Hannah. She was shaking," replied Flora sweetly.

Agnes crossed to Hannah's bedside, where the little girl was nursing a high temperature.

"You feeling unwell?" she asked.

Hannah said nothing, but thrust forward and expelled the contents of her stomach across the floor.

The child started to cry, "it's okay Hannah, don't worry I'll clean it up before the nuns see."

Hannah was new to the convent, a fragile child with a weak institution. It was usual for illness to strike down the newcomers, a regimen that those who hadn't been born in the institution suffered.

If you didn't die during that time, then you were put to work. The strong survived, the weak did not.

Suddenly the door of the dormitory opened, and Mother Superior entered looking even more bad tempered than usual.

"Flora," her voice demanded with ferocity.

Flora stiffened.

"Come with me, child," ordered the Mother, grabbing her wrist and dragging her towards the door.

"What has she done?" protested Daphne, jumping off the bed and following closely.

Mother Superior sent Daphne tumbling to the floor with a flick of her other hand. "I won't tolerate insubordination," she bellowed. "You'll spend the day in the dungeon."

Daphne was escorted from the dormitory and taken to the depths of the convent, where she was incarcerated in a small opening in the wall covered by a metal grate door. She had to curl herself into a ball to make her body fit the tightness of the space. She wore only her scratchy linen nightdress and nothing else.

It was Daphne's first time in the place the other kids referred to as the 'hole'. She'd heard about its horror, but hoped she would never experience it firsthand.

The walls were damp and slimy around her. She could hardly draw breath as she struggled for air in her crouched position. She couldn't panic, she mustn't, it would be the end of her. The sound of dripping water was her only companion, as she gripped her knees tightly and prayed for the hours to pass quickly.

A day in the 'hole' was a long time. One could easily go mad, but Daphne focused on the sweet, angelic face of Flora, who was probably facing a similar or worse fate at the hands of Mother Superior.

Flora was now sitting in front of Father Ignatius. An alcoholic, balding priest with bad breath and equally bad body odour.

"What have you done to Sister Regina?" demanded the priest, whose nose and cheeks glowed red from excessive consumption of brandy.

Flora shook her head, "nothing Father."

"Then why is Sister Regina dead?" announced Mother Superior.

Flora had no idea why elderly Sister Regina was dead. Old age seemed the pertinent answer.

"You killed her, didn't you?" demanded the Mother.

"How could she?" interrupted Sister Ophelia. "She's been locked in her dormitory all night."

"She has a point," agreed the Priest, "perhaps it was just Regina's time."

"The child is possessed," declared the Reverend Mother. "We all know it."

"If that's the case, I suggest an exorcism," slurred the Father, "though good luck getting the Diocese to agree. I don't see any evidence of possession in this girl, and that's exactly what they will want."

Mother Superior exhaled loudly, "I know you did this," she wagged an accusing finger at Flora, then abruptly left the room.

Father Ignatius looked upon the innocence of Flora's young face, the big blue eyes, the soft blond curls, "you may go child," he signalled with a wave of his hand.

Sister Ophelia lead Flora back to the dormitory.

She had seen the look on Sister Regina's face as she hesitated to discipline the girl earlier that day. The look was not of fear for the child, but of submission.

Flora was special, something that secretly confused the nun. Whatever Flora was capable of, she didn't think it was murder!

D aphne heard the sound of soft footsteps. Flora's face appeared between the bars of the metal door.

"I brought you some water," soothed Flora, placing a small flask towards Daphne's lips.

Daphne gulped at the refreshing taste. She had been alone for hours now without reprieve.

"Thank you," she smiled, tilting her face towards Flora's, "don't get caught on my behalf," cautioned Daphne, fearing for the little girl's safety.

"I won't. The nuns are at Vespers," replied Flora.

"It's that time already?" queried Daphne, hopeful of imminent release.

Vespers were taken every evening and lasted about an hour.

"What's going on upstairs? Why all the commotion earlier?" questioned Daphne, thankful for Flora's company.

"Sister Regina has died," informed Flora.

"Thank goodness," smiled Daphne, "the scourge of the kitchen is no more."

Flora giggled and nodded in agreement.

"Why did Mother Superior drag you from the dormitory then?"

"She thinks I was to blame for her death," replied Flora.

"How ridiculous," scoffed Daphne. "How could you have had anything to do with her death?"

Flora shrugged. "I don't think she likes me very much."

Daphne had to agree with Flora's statement. Mother Superior blamed Flora for anything unusual that happened at the Convent.

"She wants me to have an explosion!" added Flora innocently.

Daphne thought for a moment, "an explosion? Do you mean an exorcism?"

"Yes, that's right," nodded Flora.

Exorcism was Mother Superior's way of dealing with anything she couldn't rationally explain.

On this occasion, however, the death of the elderly Sister Regina from old age was perfectly rational, so why was exorcism mentioned? Daphne was confused. Flora was the sweetest and kindest child she had encountered. Yes, she was special, in a can't quite put my finger on it, kind of way. Daphne concluded that Mother Superior felt unnerved by the angelic Flora, hence her mistreatment of her.

Flora skipped along the corridor towards the kitchen. The smell of broth was pulling her in that direction.

Sister Ophelia stood at the stove. She had always assisted Sister Regina with cooking duties and now assumed she had been promoted to the old nun's role.

"Sit down, eat while it's hot," smiled the nun, placing a steaming pot of vegetable broth on the table. She ladled the bowls equally and watched as the children enjoyed her debut meal as the new cook.

"This is delicious," stated Agnes, licking her spoon for every last remnant.

"Can you save some for Daphne, please?" asked Flora.

The nun's face changed as her thoughts turned to Daphne locked inside the tortuous hole.

"Of course," she smiled, wrapping a bowl in cloth and placing it in the oven to stay warm.

When Daphne was finally released from her prison, she could hardly stand. The muscles in her legs were hard with cramp and every bone in her body pained with movement. Her fingers were numb with cold and her nightgown saturated from the dampness of wet stone.

When Daphne appeared in the kitchen, everyone cheered. Sister Ophelia placed a chair beside the stove for her to warm herself. Her lips were blue and she could hardly hold her bowl of broth from the shaking of her hands.

Flora was quickly there to help, spoon feeding her friend until the bowl was empty.

Sister Ophelia looked on with pride. How could the Mother Superior have dreamed that Flora had anything to do with Sister Regina's death? It just didn't make sense.

IV

Sister Regina was laid to rest in the gardens of the convent in an area set aside for faithful nuns.

Beneath the branches of a distorted olive tree, the old nun's body was interred and her resting place marked by a traditional wooden cross.

"Did you see her face?" asked Sister Grace in a whisper.

"No," replied Sister Ophelia, "why?"

Sister Grace moved closer, "I was tasked with preparing her body alongside Sister Irene," began the nun, "at first she looked tranquil, as though she were gazing upon the face of God, she was even pleasant to gaze upon, but the following morning her expression had changed. She looked in pain, excruciating pain. Her tongue had severed, her eyes were no longer milky white, but black. Her eyelids wouldn't close no matter how I tried. She wore a mask of fear as though she were now looking upon the face of the Devil."

Sister Ophelia had no words of reply, but searched for Sister Irene amongst the nuns. She would be interested to hear her version of events, as Sister Grace was prone to bouts of dramatisation.

"Where is Sister Irene?" she questioned.

The expression on Sister Grace's face grew solemn as she realised that Sister Irene had not joined them in mourning.

She grabbed Sister Ophelia's hand without explanation and pulled her along the corridor to Sister Irene's room.

She tapped gently, "Sister Irene?"

There was no response.

She tried the door, but it was locked, its key still resting in place.

Sister Grace rattled the door forcefully until the sound of the key hitting the floor could be heard. She reached beneath the gap at the bottom of the door and retrieved it, unlocking the door without hesitation and pushing it open.

Sister Ophelia looked on questioningly. Why was Sister Grace so desperate to contact Sister Irene?

Sister Grace entered the room and screamed.

Sister Irene was hanging above her bed, rope tied to the rafters, her neck so tightly bound it had almost severed, blood staining the crisp, white sheets below.

The Mother Superior heard the scream and joined them, gasping with horror at the sight of the hanging nun.

Father Ignatius staggered into the room and lowered the dead nun's body onto the bed. His face paled, his hands trembling.

They gazed at each other in stunned silence. Another nun was dead. That made two in the last two days!

Flora tiptoed amongst the graves, picking flowers to lay for the recently departed nun. She arranged the daisies and buttercups below the sister's name and smiled upon the mound of freshly turned earth that signified her resting place.

She was about to walk away when a tiny featherless bird fell to the ground in front of her. Flora looked up. A fledgling had plummeted from the nest above, its mother frantically chirping and thrashing as she searched for her missing chick.

Flora scooped the tiny body up into her hands. The bird was lifeless, not breathing.

Flora bent forward and breathed upon its tiny beak as though she were breathing new life into it and whispered something only she and the bird were privy to.

For a moment, the bird remained still, then the beak opened slowly, and the eyes fluttered to life. The fledgling climbed to its feet in the palm of her hand.

Flora climbed the tree and placed the chick back in its nest.

Had she just performed a miracle? Was it possible that the baby bird was simply stunned and not dead at all? From the distance it had fallen, it was safe to assume that it wouldn't have survived.

Flora did not know what had happened, or where the words she spoke came from. Something deep inside had compelled her to react that way, an inner voice guiding her actions from within.

The Mother Superior had witnessed the act first-hand from the window of her office. She could hardly believe what she had encountered. It marked a new revelation in the child's abilities that seemed to be growing in power. Perhaps the child would have her uses after all.

"Shouldn't we inform the police?" asked Sister Ophelia.

"And say what, a nun has committed suicide?" replied Father Ignatius, "do you really want to involve outside authorities, have them snooping around the convent? Isn't it bad enough that one of our flock has taken her own life?"

"Has she though?" growled Mother Superior.

"What do you mean by that?" queried the priest.

"Did she commit suicide or was she murdered?" declared the Mother.

Father Ignatius threw his hands in the air. "Really, do you really believe that?" he bellowed.

"There is no reason for Sister Irene to take her own life," stated the Mother Superior.

"And there is no reason to determine that she was murdered," replied the priest. "Where is your evidence?"

"Sister Grace, you were probably the last person to see her when you were preparing the body of Sister Regina. God rest her soul. How did she seem?" enquired the Holy Mother, rebuking the old priest's words.

Sister Grace hadn't really thought about it, but now that she did, she remembered how Sister Irene had been freaked out by the old nun's appearance and hadn't been able to complete the task, leaving Sister Grace to continue alone.

Should the nun reveal details of the old sister's appearance or would she be thought to have lost her mind... imagined it? Without Sister Irene to endorse the story, she chose to remain silent.

"She seemed perfectly fine," answered Sister Grace, tentatively deciding not to reveal anything more.

"Then what compelled you to pay her a visit?" questioned the Reverend Mother.

For a moment there was silence, while Sister Grace concocted a feasible story.

"She wasn't at Sister Regina's burial. I thought it out of character, thought she might be ill," revealed the nun. "I simply went to check on her."

"And you, Sister?" the Mother's eyes were now firmly planted upon Sister Ophelia.

"I was simply walking the corridor when I happened upon Sister Grace. She seemed concerned, so I accompanied her," muttered the nun.

"What are we to do?" begged Father Ignatius, anxiously rubbing his hands together, a symptom of withdrawal when he needed a fix of alcohol.

"We must keep this quiet for now," commanded the Holy Mother. "We will tell the others that Sister Irene is feeling unwell and wishes to be left alone. We will keep the door locked until I have had time to think."

Though the demands were highly irregular, the nuns obeyed and parted company to pray upon the situation and the soul of Sister Irene.

That evening, as Vespers closed and the nuns dispersed, Mother Superior headed towards the girl's dormitory.

"Flora!" she demanded in a waspish tone. "Come with me."

Flora, dressed in a white linen nightgown, padded across the floor barefoot.

"Where are you...?" began Daphne, who felt a certain sisterly duty towards the small girl.

Mother Superior gave Daphne an unnerving glare. Daphne retreated beneath the blanket of her iron framed bed and said no more. She did not care to spend another day in the dungeon.

Flora was dragged along the dimly lit corridor of the convent, jogging to keep pace with the Mother's purposeful footsteps.

She unlocked the door of Sister Irene's room and entered, pulling the girl in behind her.

Flora had never seen a dead body before and at first she thought the nun was sleeping, but the red stains on the bedsheets soon helped her realise that Sister Irene was desperately hurt.

"What's wrong with Sister Irene?" begged Flora timidly.

"She needs your help, child," replied the Mother.

Flora was pushed to the side of the bed, where the milky white stare of the nun's lifeless eyes met hers. She retreated with a gasp, her tiny body hitting the unevenness of the stone wall behind her. The nun's face was something that occurred in nightmares or the scary stories that Agnes would sometimes tell before bed. Flora began to tremble.

"Get on with it Flora, what are you waiting for?" growled Mother Superior.

Flora stared back with uncertainty. She could feel the rush of panic rising inside her and the swell of tears gathering. How could she help Sister Irene? She had no idea what to do.

She glanced towards the Holy Mother with a questioning expression.

"Do what you did to the bird!" commanded Mother Superior, her gaze as ferocious as her words, "I saw you this afternoon in the graveyard. You saved the fallen bird, performed some sort of miracle."

Miracle! Flora didn't understand the word, nor how the baby bird had recovered from its fall. All she had done was breathe on the stillness of its tiny beak and whisper upon it. Perhaps that was what the Mother Superior was talking about.

Flora hesitated, then moving slowly, she bent over the nun until her cheek was almost touching Sister Irene's deathly cold skin. She closed her eyes, afraid of the closeness, and breathed just as she had on the bird.

She stepped quickly away from the body and waited, but the nun remained lifeless.

"Do it again!" demanded Mother Superior.

Flora wanted to decline the request, but she knew that in doing so she would face a worst fate. Perhaps a week in the 'hole'. She shuddered at the thought. Somehow, almost kissing the face of the death ridden nun didn't seem so bad in comparison.

Flora closed her eyes and waited. Suddenly, she felt it. That feeling deep inside, like a shadow rising out of the darkness. The same feeling she'd had in the graveyard. Something her innocent mind could not understand.

She moved forward and repeated the ritual, but still the nun didn't move.

"Perhaps it only works on birds," mumbled Flora without daring to meet the Mother's eyes.

Mother Superior pushed Flora to one side and felt at the dead nun's wrist.

She grabbed the child by the hand and pushed her out into the corridor. "Wait there," she commanded, closing the door.

Moments later, a scream trembled from Sister Irene's room as the Mother Superior, as pale faced as the dead nun, opened the door and signalled to Flora.

Flora stepped forward cautiously as the door opened fully, catching sight of Sister Irene, who was sitting upright on the bed.

"You did it, child," announced Mother Superior, signing herself with the cross. "Sister Irene is alive!"

VI

The convent sprang to life around 5am each morning with breakfast being the first order of the day.

The nuns ate at a separate table to the orphaned children, often leaving early to commence prayers.

That morning, everyone was still seated when Sister Irene entered the room. No-one noticed her at first, except for Sister Ophelia, who almost dropped her breakfast bowl, and Sister Grace, who almost fainted with shock.

Both drained of colour as Sister Irene took her place at the table, unaware of the distress her presence induced.

Mother Superior continued as though the previously dead nun's presence was not worthy of comment.

It was Father Ignatius who broke the silence as he stumbled into the kitchen for much needed coffee, which he instantly poured down himself as his eyes met with those of Sister Irene.

"What's the matter Father, you look like you've seen a ghost?" questioned the nun.

"It cannot be!" bellowed the priest. "You're dead, I saw you..."

"That's quite enough, Father," interrupted Mother Superior, "you've overdosed on the whisky again." Taking him by the arm, she led him from the room.

Father Ignatius stared over his shoulder, disbelieving his own eyes and protesting his sobriety.

Sister Irene, unperturbed by the priests' comments, continued to eat whilst the other nuns looked on curiously.

In the confines of her office, the Mother Superior attempted to calm the old priest.

"Isn't it wonderful Father, a miracle has occurred within these very walls? Divine intervention from our Lord himself," began the Mother, "St. Catharine's will become a holy place of pilgrimage and you Father will most certainly earn the title of Bishop."

Father Ignatius ceased protesting as the Mother's words were absorbed.

"But, I saw with my own eyes, clouded by whisky or not, Sister Irene was dead," he protested.

"That's why her resurrection is such a miracle," comforted the Reverend Mother. "St. Catharine's has been truly blessed."

Father Ignatius needed a brandy. How could it be that the hanging nun, whose head had almost severed by her restraint, was eating breakfast in the kitchen? It was not possible, unless, as the Holy Mother pointed out, a miracle had taken place. Father Ignatius had never witnessed a miracle before, but he had witnessed the forces of evil.

He gulped at his brandy, fearing the latter was the more plausible answer.

Sister Ophelia and Sister Grace could not finish their food, the unnerving presence of Sister Irene had turned their stomachs. They headed to Mother Superior's office. Father Ignatius had rooted himself in the comfy seat by the window as they entered.

"Close the door," commanded Mother Superior. "I know why you're both here."

Before either nun could speak, the Mother continued, "a miracle has blessed our convent, sisters. God himself has chosen Sister Irene as his vessel of divine provenance."

The nuns were both stunned by the revelation. Both were unconvinced.

"Sister Irene was dead, hanging by the neck. We all saw her. How can it be that she is eating breakfast in the kitchen?" questioned Sister Ophelia.

"My thoughts exactly," added the old priest.

"Has your faith abandoned you, Sister?" replied the Reverend Mother fiercely. "Are you questioning God's miracle?"

Sister Ophelia could not answer, could not rationalise the Holy Mother's words.

"Our friend Lazarus has fallen asleep, but now I will go and wake him up, John 11," recited Father Ignatius, hiccuping between words, "when Jesus performed that miracle Lazarus had been dead for four days."

"Yes thank you Father, we are all well versed in the Bible," scolded Mother Superior.

"Ah yes, but," slurred the priest, "Lazarus had not almost been beheaded."

Mother Superior was not amused as she turned to the nuns, "you should pray on this, sisters. I fear your faith may be failing you."

The nuns headed towards the chapel. Both feeling uncomfortable, both harbouring doubts about Sister Irene's sudden return from the dead.

"I feel like I'm living in a horror movie, not that I've ever seen one, but I imagine this is what it's like," babbled Sister Grace, "I shall be locking my bedroom door tonight and sleeping with my rosary. Might even say extra prayers before bed."

"It is unnerving," replied Sister Ophelia. "I think we should keep an eye on Sister Irene. Something about this 'miracle' is deceiving. Mother Superior is holding back on the facts."

That day they trailed the reborn Sister Irene, watching from a distance as she carried out her duties with normalcy. She looked like Sister Irene and she moved like Sister Irene, with that awkward hip movement caused by arthritic disease on her left side. She spoke like Sister Irene, but there was an emptiness within her eyes as though her soul had not returned with her.

A couple of days passed. Sister Irene continued her daily routine just as before her miraculous resurrection.

It was a month later, on the way to Vespers, that Sister Grace noticed Sister Irene's hands were dripping blood. Her rosary was covered, yet the sister herself seemed not to have noticed.

"Sister, your hands," declared Sister Grace.

The nun gazed upon the bright red liquid that oozed from her palms. She raised her face to the light as droplets of blood ran down her cheeks, and a growing pool beneath her habit left imprints from the soles of her sandals as she walked.

The Reverend Mother seemed unperturbed by the discovery, throwing her hands into the air, praising the Lord.

"What does this mean?" questioned Sister Grace as the flow of blood increased.

"These are the signs of the stigmata," revealed the Mother Superior, "the wounds inflicted on Jesus himself at his crucifixion. Only God's chosen ones receive this miracle! Don't you see? This endorses my belief that Sister Irene has been chosen by God."

Sister Irene was bundled away, her wounds cleaned and dressed. From that moment on, she wore bandages around her hands and feet and bore the marks of unhealed scars around her forehead.

"I imagine you will be Sainted," declared the Reverend Mother as she sat at Sister Irene's bedside one evening.

Tears flowed readily from the nun, themselves stained red. She had paled through the constant loss of blood, her eyes sunken and dark. Sister Irene was fading slowly away.

"Now, now, Sister, you have been chosen by God himself. What greater honour can there be than for a nun to receive the stigmata?"

"It feels more of a curse than an honour," replied Sister Irene. "I don't feel myself. Something is taking over my body, and it isn't God."

Mother Superior would hear no more of the ungrateful nun's protestations. She thrust the rosary into her hand. "Pray, Sister, to the Lord who granted you such a miracle, remember your faith, your vows. Pray until you do!"

Father Ignatius, during a spell of sobriety, called upon the ailing nun.

"Sister, I fear you have been marked, but not by God," he confessed.

The nun nodded her agreement, "help me Father. Grant me absolution," she pleaded.

"If only it were that easy, my child," answered the priest with a solemn tone.

He had noticed a darkness following Sister Irene, an unearthly shadow attached to her, a malignant stench that lingered as she passed, and how the flowers she planted wilted beneath her touch. Father Ignatius had seen these signs before, perhaps more times than he cared to remember.

"The disease inside you grows stronger each day. I would need approval from the Diocese to help you, but I fear time is not on our side Sister, to wait for that would be too late."

"Then do what you must, Father, please," begged the nun.

Father Ignatius knew the toll of exorcism. He was no longer strong enough to uphold the aggression it demanded, and he knew that Sister Irene was too frail. It would mean certain death for one or both of them.

"I cannot risk it, Sister. I wish my answer were different. I'm afraid that only God can save you now. Pray for yourself and I shall pray for you."

The following day, Sister Irene was struggling to walk. The pain in her feet had increased and the blood flow was relentless. Her sandals pinched from the bulk of bandages and her body ached like never before.

She knelt to dig potatoes in the garden; they withered beneath her touch. She wept tears of blood and abandoned the chore, stumbling towards the graveyard, where she rested against the twisted trunk of an olive tree, gasping to draw breath. Her body ached with pain. There was no release. Surely God would not want her to suffer in this way? She began to pray.

It happened so quickly, all she could remember was the grasp of a hand around her ankle, cold bony fingers holding her firmly in place as a small bird flew viciously towards her. It attacked with the ferocity of a vulture and the strength of an eagle, yet it was no bigger than a sparrow, pecking at her eyeballs, tearing at the skin. She was too weak to fight it off.

There wasn't time to scream between the incessant attacks. She fell to the ground, disturbing the earth of Sister Agnes' burial plot. Deathly arms folded around her. Skeletal, putrid, rotten flesh securing her in place as the bird continued its attack.

It was Flora who discovered her, lying dead beneath the olive tree, eyes gauged from their sockets, blood enveloping her face. The expression of shock painted her death mask, tongue almost severed from the clench of her teeth.

A dribble of something wet grazed Flora's cheek. She looked up to find a small bird looking down from the branch of the tree, blood dripping from the end of its beak. She knew it was the chick she had saved. It squawked loudly at her before flying away.

Flora screamed. The nuns gathered. The scene was gruesome. Sister Irene was dead... Again!

VII

In the aftermath of the nun's death, unease spread through the convent. Prayer time increased as everyone felt a darkness creeping the halls of the holy cloister. There were many unanswered questions and no explanation for Sister Irene's untimely and disturbing demise!

In the shadows of the dimly lit corridors, a shadowy figure stalked the darkness. Everyone had seen it but no one dare to speak of it, clasping their rosaries and uttering prayers of protection as they hurried to their rooms in fear.

Father Ignatius fell into a drunken stupor, hardly leaving the confines of his quarters. He took confession on the odd occasion, falling asleep before administering absolution. The Mother

Superior prayed constantly and the more she prayed, the darker the cloud that enveloped the convent.

On the morning of Flora's seventh birthday, Mother Superior declared the child must leave the convent for good.

"But where will she go?" begged Sister Ophelia. "Has a family come forward for her?"

"No, but she cannot stay here," affirmed the Holy Mother.

"I don't understand. What has she done to rile you so?"

The Mother Superior sighed heavily. "She has brought a curse upon us, Sister. She and only she is responsible for Sister Irene's death."

"But how can that be? She's nothing but an innocent child?" replied Sister Ophelia.

"A child maybe, but innocent; she is not."

"What do you mean?" pressed the nun. "How can she possibly be responsible for Sister Irene's death?"

The Mother Superior, realising Sister Ophelia's fondness for the child, breathed deeply. "It was Flora who brought Sister Irene to life," she revealed.

It took a moment for her words to absorb as Sister Ophelia sank into the nearest chair.

Her expression still questioning, her mouth slightly agape.

"You knew she was different, you felt it, didn't you?" demanded the Mother.

Sister Ophelia could not deny that her feelings for Flora ran deep. She saw something in the child that the other children lacked, something mysterious that Flora's innocence had not yet discovered.

"You asked her to do it?" queried the nun.

Mother Superior nodded.

"How could you know she was capable of such a thing?"

"I saw her revive a bird that had fallen from its nest. It was a miracle, or so I thought. I hoped she could use her gift, though I use the word loosely, on Sister Irene."

"How could you presume to do such a thing?" questioned the nun.

"To save this convent from the shame of suicide," hissed the Reverend Mother.

"Your motive was pride!" declared Sister Ophelia.

"My motive was the untimely death of Sister Irene," came the reply.

Sister Ophelia shook her head dubiously. "If it were God's will that Sister Irene should live, then so be it, but this was not God's work. There was no divine intervention, and you knew. All this time you knew. You have brought a darkness upon our convent."

"No!" bellowed the Holy Mother. "Flora has done that. We are living under her curse. The child must go tonight!"

VIIII

The hour was early as Sister Ophelia interrupted Flora's sleep. "Come child," she whispered, pulling Flora to an upright position.

The nun had already packed a small bag with all that Flora possessed, which wasn't much at all.

They crept into the night without explanation and left the convent in a waiting taxi.

It was Flora's first time away from the convent. She had been born there and sheltered within its walls ever since. There was little to see through the darkness of the hour, and sleep deprived her of even that.

"We're here," declared Sister Ophelia, lifting Flora's tired body from the vehicle.

They had stopped outside a house; the door was open, and a woman waited on the steps of the porch.

"What's going on?" questioned the woman as Sister Ophelia passed her without a word.

Inside, she placed Flora on the sofa and took the woman aside.

"This is the emergency I spoke of," began Ophelia.

"A child!" groaned the woman.

"Please, she has nowhere else to go and I fear for her safety if she remains another day at the convent," pleaded the nun.

"Why? What has she done?"

"Nothing, but Mother Superior has taken a dislike to her. She wants the child gone, no matter what."

The woman eyed Flora, who was dozing against the cushions.

"She looks harmless enough, I suppose. I'll take her for a few days. In the meantime, you must find her a more permanent home."

Sister Ophelia agreed. She kissed the sleeping Flora and placed a rosary in her hands. "Stay safe, little one," she muttered as she left.

Flora awoke in a sunlit bedroom, snuggled beneath the warmth of a fluffy duvet and wearing soft, sweet-smelling pyjamas. For a moment she thought it to be a dream, but then she realised there was another child beside her.

"Daphne?" she questioned. It wasn't Daphne. The girl was a stranger, slightly bigger than her, with dark brown hair.

The child began to wake, opening her eyes and smiling.

"You must be Flora?" she began.

Flora nodded timidly.

"I'm Amelia," giggled the girl, who then bounced out of bed and pulled on her slippers.

"Do you have any?" she questioned, pointing at the fluffy pink coverings on her feet.

Flora shook her head.

Amelia disappeared into a cupboard and returned with a similar pair in blue decorated with velvet bows.

She placed them beside Flora. "Here, you can wear these. I don't use them anymore."

Flora smiled and climbed out of bed.

"Follow me," shouted Amelia as she disappeared from the bedroom, leading Flora downstairs to the kitchen area.

"Want breakfast?"

Flora nodded.

"Okay, we've got cereal, toast, waffles, pancakes, croissants, bacon or eggs?"

Flora hesitated. She hadn't heard of most of the listed foods other than cereal and toast and porridge on a special occasion, like a religious holiday.

"I'll surprise you," declared Amelia, who seemed happy to have a breakfast companion.

"What are you up to?" asked a woman's voice entering the kitchen.

"Making breakfast, silly," replied Amelia.

Flora vaguely recognised the woman, remembering her talking with Sister Ophelia the night before.

"I'm Orla," introduced the woman. "Ophelia is my sister and I'm also Amelia's mammy," she explained with a smile. "You'll be staying with us for a couple of days."

"YAY!" exploded Amelia, throwing cereal across the table in her excitement.

As breakfast ended, Flora began gathering the dirty dishes.

"It's okay. You don't have to do that here," explained Orla.

Really, thought Flora, no chores. What kind of convent is this?

That first day was spent like no other Flora had ever experienced. Amelia dressed her in jeans and t-shirt, gave her some trainers to wear and lead her to the car.

They drove to a market where Orla and Amelia shopped for clothes. They even bought Flora a new outfit and her own pyjamas. Then stopped off for lunch, followed by ice cream and an afternoon spent in the park. It was the best day of Flora's short life.

That night, Flora overheard Orla on the telephone.

"What about school?" she heard her say. Flora was no stranger to school, lessons were carried out each day by Sister Catherine and Sister Mercy.

"Well, how much longer?" questioned Orla, obviously displeased by the reply.

"I suppose it will have to be okay, but I'll have to enrol her in school. I can't keep taking days off work."

A couple of days later, Flora was accompanying Amelia to junior school.

There were lots of children everywhere, some bigger, some smaller than she. The noise was overwhelming at first, but after a couple of days, Flora settled and began looking forward to attending class.

Living with Orla and Amelia was wonderful, as the days turned into weeks, and the weeks into months.

Sister Ophelia had failed to find anywhere else for Flora to live. She was becoming very much a part of the family, and she loved it.

The week before the Christmas holidays, Orla brought home a rescue dog. A great big fluffy, black and white hound that loved licking and sniffing and playing ball in the garden.

"I've been meaning to get a dog for ages," explained Orla. "Now just seemed like the right time. He's a Christmas present to us."

They named him Rocky.

The new year approached, and school began again. Rocky was always waiting, wagging his tail with excitement when they arrived home. He was a loving dog, excessive with his delegation of kisses from an overactive tongue and desperate for tummy tickles and fuss.

Then it happened. Amelia and Flora had followed the ice-cream van down the street to buy lollies. Rocky was waiting by the roadside for them to return. The moment he spotted them on the other side of the street, he raced forward, crossing the road into the path of a speeding car. The dog was crushed beneath the wheels of the vehicle that failed to stop. Amelia was distraught. Rocky was dead, but Flora knew exactly what to do.

She closed her eyes and waited. Then leaned towards the blood-soaked canine and breathed on him. This time she was taking no chances, so she breathed again, just like the Mother Superior had asked her to do for Sister Irene.

"What are you doing?" sobbed Amelia.

Flora didn't reply. She waited for the dark shadow inside her to subside.

After a few minutes, Rocky started breathing. He stood up, shook himself down and snuggled into the waiting arms of a startled Amelia.

Orla had witnessed the act from her porch. It sent an icy shiver coasting her spine. She couldn't believe what had happened. There was no way that Rocky could have survived such an accident, but there he was, covered in blood and chasing his tail playfully.

Orla took him to the vets just to be certain. X-ray revealed that almost every bone in the dog's body had been fractured, but also that every bone had healed instantly.

"Are you certain he was hit by a car?" queried the vet, baffled by the extent of injury Rocky's X-rays had revealed.

Orla nodded. "I was there, saw it! I thought the dog was most certainly dead."

The vet shook his head, "these broken bones can't possibly have occurred today," he declared, "it takes weeks for them to heal from an impact like this, that is, if the dog survived at all. These must be old fractures."

"Do they look like old fractures?" demanded Orla.

The vet took another look and frowned. He couldn't explain the newness of the healed fractures. It was something he had never witnessed in his thirty years of experience.

"Well, I suppose he's a very lucky boy," declared the vet.

Orla smiled nervously. She had the answer she expected. Flora had performed a miracle in front of her eyes. Perhaps she was beginning to understand why the nuns had cast her aside. Whatever Flora was capable of, Orla suspected, was not God given.

Amelia, on the other hand, was just happy to have her canine friend back. She didn't question how it had happened or look at Flora any differently, other than with gratitude, but Orla did!

IX

"I'm telling you, Ophelia, I saw her bring the dog back to life, right there in the middle of the street," declared Orla down the telephone.

Sister Ophelia didn't seem surprised and answered with silence.

"You're not shocked, are you? You already knew that she was capable of such things?" demanded Orla.

Sister Ophelia couldn't deny it. Her thoughts were in turmoil.

She wanted to warn her sister to keep a good eye on the dog, but then, if she did, it would most likely jeopardise Flora's place in the home. If she said nothing, there was no telling what might happen with the dog in the next days, weeks, even months.

If it were to follow the same path as Sister Irene, then she couldn't bear to think of what lay ahead.

"Is that why she had to leave the convent? She's done this before?" pleaded Orla.

Sister Ophelia hesitated long enough for her to have the answer.

"She doesn't know what she's capable of Orla, it's done out of innocence. She obviously wanted to soothe Amelia's distress. She means no harm."

"I'm sorry, but you need to find her somewhere else to live and sooner rather than later," warned Orla. "I mean it this time. She has to go!"

Sister Ophelia begged for a little more time, appealing to her sister's better nature, and was finally granted an extra week.

"That's final," scolded Orla, "no longer than a week! Do you hear me?"

Unfortunately, a week could be too long, anything might happen!

When Amelia arrived home from school that day, she threw down her school bag as usual and headed straight towards Rocky for a 'missed you' cuddle.

She'd thought it odd that the dog wasn't waiting for her by the door. It was the first time since he'd lived with them he hadn't shown up. Nevertheless, she threw her arms around the muscular shoulders of her pet and squeezed lovingly. Rocky usually loved the attention, nuzzling her with his wet nose and licking her face excitedly, except for today. Rocky didn't reciprocate, instead, he did quite the opposite. Baring his teeth and snarling, lip curled threateningly as he fixed his stare on a shocked Amelia.

"What's wrong Rocky?" questioned the little girl, her lip beginning to quiver, "don't you love me anymore?"

Amelia took a step backwards as the snarling increased. Rocky displayed a mouthful of razor sharp canines gnashing ferociously, saliva dripping from the corners of his mouth. Amelia was too afraid to move.

Flora was in the kitchen unpacking her schoolbag, and Orla was busy making dinner. The lounge was not visible from there, neither were aware of Amelia's plight.

A high-pitched, tortuous scream echoed through the house, bringing both of them racing into the living room, where Amelia lay wrestling with the strength of the dog, as it flung her viciously around the room with the ease of a rag doll.

Rocky had locked his jaws across Amelia's tiny face, tearing at the flesh, stripping it from the bone effortlessly. Amelia made a bid for freedom as the dog released her momentarily, then lunged again, this time sinking its teeth into the side of her neck. Blood pooled on the carpet beneath as she spluttered and choked beneath its jaws. Orla kicked and punched at the animal, sending him reeling to one side, but it was too late. Amelia's carotid artery had been severed in the attack and she was already dead before Orla reached her.

Flora watched as Orla cradled her child and shrieked with distress. At that moment, she felt nothing. No empathy, no sadness. Only emptiness.

The volume of noise had alerted their neighbour, who barged into the room, where Amelia's blood decorated the carpet.

Rocky had skulked off to a corner of the room where he died quietly before authorities arrived to do the job for him.

Amelia's death would be attributed to a dangerous dog incident, but Orla knew the truth. How would she explain it to a professional? They'd have her locked up in no time. She saw Flora leave the room. It was the last time she saw her.

Flora accompanied the kindly neighbour to his home, whilst Orla was escorted to the police station. There were formalities to take care of.

Flora somehow knew that her presence would no longer be welcome in the house she had adopted as home. After all, Orla would not want to be reminded of her daughter's horrific death, something that Flora's existence would conjure daily.

Flora would leave before the grieving mother returned, where she would go she did not know.

X

In the aftermath of Amelia's death, Orla gave little thought to the whereabouts of Flora. She knew the child had disappeared on the evening she returned from the police station and if she were being honest; she felt relieved.

Since Flora's arrival in her home, she had lost her only child. Flora, with her expressive blue eyes and angelic demeanour, was responsible for everything. The child harboured a darkness, masked beneath her endearing appearance. There had been no witnesses to Flora's miraculous act nor to the sudden personality change in an otherwise passive, friendly dog, but Orla was certain both tragedies were somehow related to Flora.

"Where is she?" demanded Sister Ophelia when she learned of Flora's departure.

"I don't know and don't care," replied Orla between sobs.

"How could Flora have had anything to do with Amelia's death?" quizzed the nun, who deep down had worried that such an event was possible.

"I think you know how. You knew when you asked me to take her in!" snarled Orla. "She belongs in an institution away from society, so she can't hurt anyone else."

Sister Ophelia remained silent. She couldn't deny that Flora was indeed special, but the child was innocent.She had no conscious knowledge that her actions would end in tragedy. Flora's intentions were pure of heart. The nun was sure of that.

Sister Ophelia requested compassionate leave to attend her niece's funeral and search for the missing child.

Flora had left the neighbour's house by the back exit. The man was enveloped by sleep stretched out beside the glare of a tv screen, an empty bottle of beer befriending him. He'd been unaware of her presence for a while. He wouldn't hear her slip out of the door and into the wilderness beyond.

The grass was so long it touched Flora's waist as she waded forward in the dark.

She hit a gravel path and followed its trail. Trekking through field after field until she reached the summit of a hill and looked back upon the brightly lit neighbourhood below.

She sat for a moment, catching her breath. Listening to the stillness of the night. Aware that she was totally alone and cold.

She reached into her pocket and pulled out a chocolate bar. The kindly old neighbour had given it to her earlier that evening. She nibbled at it cautiously, aware that it was her only source of food.

Strange noises behind her made her stiffen, dropping the remains of her snack into the long grass. Flora had never been further than the graveyard of the convent. Sitting alone in the openness of vast countryside with only the moon as company made her feel afraid. Her thoughts turned to Daphne, who no doubt was already nestled beneath the paper-thin sheets of her dormitory bed. Flora longed for that security and for Daphne's friendship once again. She would go back to the convent, to Daphne, who would look after her.

As a breeze whipped coolly around her, Flora headed towards the cover of trees in the distance. She would sleep here for tonight and then in the morning she would set off in search of St. Catharine's.

Flora was awoken by raucous laughing, a woman's voice out in the clearing. She unfolded herself slowly, twigs and leaves decorating her clothes and curls as she crept from the warmth of her tree root bed.

She heard it again. Flora headed towards the sound at the edge of the woodland and the open expanse of meadow beyond it. A woman was throwing a ball for her dog, who was chasing enthusiastically, retrieving and bringing back attentively as the woman laughed. She wore a brightly coloured scarf around her hair and a long green coat that was flapping in the breeze.

Suddenly, the dog's attention changed as it caught the child's scent and headed in Flora's direction. Flora, soiled by remnants of her dirt bed, stood firm as the dog approached. It stopped a short distance away and began barking loudly.

The dog's owner approached. "What have you found, Toby?" asked the woman as she headed towards her canine friend.

The woman was heavily made up with bright red lips and overstated eyelashes. She observed Flora suspiciously looking her up and down, then glancing around the area.

"What are you doing out here? Are you alone?" she questioned.

Flora nodded.

"Where's your mammy?"

Flora shrugged.

"Do you have a name?"

"Flora."

"Have you been out here all night, Flora?" enquired the woman, dusting leaves and dirt from her clothing.

Flora shrugged again.

The woman held out her hand, "come Flora, I'll take you to someone who can find your mammy."

Flora didn't bother informing her rescuer that it would be impossible; she didn't know who her mother was, or even if she had one.

The dog continued to bark, side eyeing Flora along every inch of the journey, ensuring it walked on the opposite side of the pavement to the child. The woman protested harshly, but the dog ignored her.

She lead Flora along the high street, stopping at a small cafe, where Flora ate breakfast. The dog cowered at its owner's feet, hiding between the legs of her chair. Whimpering when Flora offered a slice of bacon, refusing to accept it.

The woman frowned. "What on earth is wrong with you, Toby? You love bacon. I do hope you're not coming down with something."

The dog wasn't ill; it was simply intuitive; it knew the child's secret.

Next stop was a large building lined with nothing but windows. Even the door seemed to be a large window.

It smelled funny inside, much like Sister Regina and Sister Irene before they died. Perhaps it was a small convent, thought Flora, though the man's uniform looked nothing like the robes that Father Ignatius wore.

Flora was too small to see over the desk, or witness the man who was talking, but he sounded nothing like the old priest, nor did he slur his words.

"Found her, you say?" repeated the man, "on Heather Bank. No place for a child to be wandering alone."

"Precisely," answered the woman, "that's why I thought it best to bring her here."

"I'll have a woman officer look after her," declared the man. "You can leave her with me now, miss. Thank you for bringing her in we will make sure she is looked after."

The young woman stooped over Flora, the smell of her strong cologne stinging the back of Flora's throat, "you're safe here, the police will find your mammy," she explained with a smile.

And with that, the woman and her lachrymose mongrel disappeared from sight.

XI

Sister Ophelia had been granted leave and had settled in at her sister Orla's home.

"Still no sign of her!" sighed the nun despondently.

Orla shrugged. "You here for Amelia or that child?" she growled sarcastically.

"Come now, you know I'm here for Amelia and you, but I can't help feeling responsible for Flora. I just need to ring the local hospital and police station, see if she's turned up."

Orla didn't reply, sipping from her mug in silence.

Sister Ophelia tried the closest hospital, but they had no record of Flora being admitted. In one way, it was a relief, but in another, it did nothing to dispel her fears for Flora's safety.

The police switchboard was constantly busy. Sister Ophelia despaired, gave up, and hurried in its direction.

The desk sergeant took down details, but stopped writing as the nun's description continued.

"I think we might have your girl here, Sister, but I can't release her into your care without paperwork," stated the police man.

"What sort of paperwork?" puzzled the nun.

"Surely she's registered with St. Catharine's Convent?"

Sister Ophelia hesitated. She had removed Flora from the convent without a thought for the relevant paperwork.

Mother Superior had wanted her gone as soon as possible and the nun had had to improvise. She couldn't ask the Reverend Mother's blessing to bring the child back. She already knew what the answer would be.

"I haven't anything with me," sighed Sister Ophelia, "but I can get it."

"That's fine," replied the sergeant. "You bring the paperwork and I'll release the child."

"So, what happens to her in the meantime?" pleaded the nun, knowing that locating the appropriate documents may take some time.

"She'll be held in temporary care for the time being," reported the policeman.

Sister Ophelia left disheartened.

Flora took a ride in a taxi accompanied by a short, rotund woman with ruby red cheeks.

"Here we are, deary," she declared as the car stopped in front of a brightly coloured house. "This is where you'll be staying for a little while."

Flora accepted her fate readily. She couldn't spend another night alone in the dark, and finding the convent would not be as easy as she'd thought. She longed for food and a warm bed. The convent and Daphne would just have to wait.

The house was smaller than it looked and crowded with people and children. The owner had a penchant for ornaments, pictures and a thirst for garish decor.

"This way," ordered the woman who had met them at the entrance, "you'll be sharing with Katrina, Alexis and Amrita."

The room was cramped, four beds filled the tiny space, with one set of drawers and a cupboard behind the door.

Flora stepped forward timidly, just as she had when being shown to a prospective family back at the convent.

"Come Mitra, this will be your bed," pointed the girl with pale brown skin and matching eyes. She brushed slender fingers through hair the colour of midnight and smiled.

Flora felt confused. Mitra wasn't her name, but the girl insisted on calling it her.

"Don't worry, she calls everyone Mitra," declared another girl who was lounging across the furthest bed reading a magazine.

"Mitra means friend where I come from," explained Amrita, pulling Flora towards the bed, "this is where I sleep and you can sleep right next to me."

"Whoopee!" cried the other girl. "Good luck with that. She snores like a wild boar."

Amrita cast her a disapproving sideways glance, "don't listen to Alexis. Let me help you unpack," declared Amrita. "Where are your bags?"

"I don't have any," muttered Flora.

Alexis laughed out loud, "nothing for you to steal Rita, how disappointed you must be."

"Pay no attention to her," demanded the Indian girl, "she forgets I know where she hides her cigarettes."

Alexis flipped over on the bed, turning to face the wall and remained silent for the rest of the afternoon.

Amrita, who preferred the shortened version of her name Rita, gave Flora a tour of her new home. It was a little dishevelled in places and harboured a distasteful smell, but it was warm and cosy in a way that Flora had never felt before.

The garden was enormous and housed a climbing frame, swings, slide, sandpit, see saw and paddling pool.

"This is the most spacious room, the garden," declared Rita, pulling Flora towards an empty swing.

"Sit down, I'll push you."

Flora obeyed, and before long, she was swinging through the air like a bird. She decided she would enjoy living here.

At dinnertime, the table was set for ten, seven children and three adults. Mr and Mrs Moreton owned the house, which they shared with Adam, their teenage son. The other occupants were children from all walks of life who, for one reason or another, had ended up in care.

Mrs Moreton, also known as Mrs M, had prepared a feast of chicken, broccoli and carrots with a side bowl of fresh homemade chips.

"Help yourself, Flora," she instructed, as the offering rapidly disappeared into hungry stomachs.

Flora had never seen so much food, nor watched it being devoured so readily.

"Speed is of the essence around this table," declared Adam with a grin.

"Apple pie!" shouted a chubby, red-headed boy as Mrs M deposited the plate in front of him.

"Your favourite Rory, so you can dish out," commanded Mrs M handing him a knife, "be fair mind, everyone gets the same amount."

Rory sliced into the dessert with care and delivered a healthy sized portion to everyone. It was the most delicious thing that Flora had ever tasted.

Flora felt happy. She could eat as much as she wanted without the eagle eyes of the nuns restricting her. She got hot chocolate and cookies at bedtime. The other children were friendly and the bed she slept in felt like she was floating on a cloud. There were no lumps or hard bits beneath the mattress poking at her ribs or squeaking when she turned. The sheets were soft, thick, and smelled of lavender.

Flora fell asleep with a smile of contentment.

XII

Amelia's funeral was a sad affair. The sight of her small white coffin disappearing beneath the earth sent Orla into a fit of hysteria. Sister Ophelia felt negligible. She questioned her God for allowing the death of her young niece. It was easier to blame him than accept the responsibility herself.

She hugged her sister closely and prayed for the soul of sweet Amelia, hugging her rosary tightly as she endeavoured to console the distraught mother.

Afterwards, Orla retreated to her bedroom and refused to mingle amongst mourners. The nun was left to entertain guests, something of which she had no previous experience.

In the kitchen, a smartly dressed man was elbow deep in dirty dishes.

"Thank you for your assistance," declared Sister Ophelia.

The man smiled and offered his rather wet and soapy hand towards her. "I'm Edward, Edward Trent."

Sister Ophelia laughed at the soapy hand and without grasping it replied, "Sister Ophelia, Orla's sister."

"I thought as much," replied the man. "I could detect a family resemblance."

"It's the nose," remarked the nun. "Everyone in the family has the same nose."

Edward smirked, "at least you didn't get these ears... I'm certain I have some elephant DNA in me!"

Sister Ophelia felt comfortable with the man, though it had been many years since she had conversed with a member of the opposite sex, with the exception of Father Ignatius.

Edward was handsome, tall with a charming demeanour and very charismatic. He made it easy for the nun to gravitate towards him.

"Terrible accident, your niece, and so young," continued Edward.

"The worst," replied Sister Ophelia. "I don't know how my sister will get through it."

"Faith perhaps?"

The nun shook her head. "I'm afraid even that has abandoned her. She was never devout, but she did once believe."

There was a moment of pause as the nun contemplated her sister's demise from the church. Perhaps it had something to do with the priest who had been accused of misconduct with members of his younger congregation. It was a topic of conversation that Orla avoided at all cost leading Sister Ophelia to believe that her own sister had been subjected to the disgraced father's advances.

"I think that's the last of it," stated Edward, draining the sink of dirty dishwater.

Sister Ophelia felt almost disappointed that their conversation had come to an end. She glanced around the room. Most people had already left except for the neighbours who were chatting happily in one corner of the dining area.

"Can I offer you a coffee as a thank you for your help?" declared the nun.

"That would be lovely, though I'd prefer something a little stronger if you have it," instructed Edward.

"A night cap! I think I can do that," replied Sister Ophelia, crossing to a small glass cabinet. "Brandy or Whiskey?"

"I'll take a brandy please," thanked Edward.

They moved to the comfort of the sofa, where Sister Ophelia removed her shoes and rubbed at her toes. The ill-fitting footwear had squeezed and pinched at her skin, her penance for not buying the appropriate size.

"What is it that you do, Edward?" asked the nun, realising that she was displaying part of her undergarment to a man she had literally just met.

"I'm a professor at the university," replied Edward, without giving away too much detail.

"A professor of what exactly?" probed the nun.

"Psychology, parapsychology and the occult. I'm your arch enemy I suppose, everything that you believe in, I believe the opposite."

Sister Ophelia pondered his words.

"You mean you believe in the Devil?"

"Don't you? Doesn't the Bible talk of such a beast, the fallen angel who opposes God?"

"So you believe in God too?"

"As a deity, yes. I'm not religious by any stretch of the imagination, but surely one cannot exist without the other?" he declared.

Sister Ophelia digested his words momentarily before asking, "do you believe that evil can exist, for example, in a newborn child?"

"I never close my mind to the possibility of anything," replied Edward, eyeing the nun with interest. "Do you know of such a child?"

Sister Ophelia shook her head and felt for the safety of her rosary. "Not exactly."

"We are all born of innocence, Sister. It very much depends upon our social and psychological interactions as to whether we remain as such."

The nun became thoughtful.

"You don't agree?" queried the professor.

"In theory, yes, but what if a child grows up in a convent surrounded by God's worship, hearing nothing but His word and speaking to him in prayer?"

"Are you speaking hypothetically now, Sister?"

Sister Ophelia wasn't sure she should elaborate. Flora was foremost in her thoughts and she felt it may be helpful to gain the man's professional opinion.

"As it happens, I do know of such a child. A little girl with eyes the colour of the bluest ocean and hair like spun gold. Her innocence knows nothing of evil, and yet I fear there may be a malevolence within her. She is yet unaware of."

Edward's expression changed. This subject had sparked his interest. "Mind if I help myself to another?" he asked, raising the empty brandy glass in the air.

"Help yourself," replied Sister Ophelia.

"Can I interest you?"

The nun shook her head.

Edward resumed his position on the sofa, though this time he sat a little closer.

"I'm intrigued Sister, please elaborate on this sinful child."

The hours skipped by with ease as the professor and the nun continued to converse. She didn't remember him leaving or how many brandies he had poured. In fact, she didn't remember much of the evening at all.

It was the bright declaration of morning that awoke her, still seated in the same position on the sofa as the night before. The mourners had dispersed, including Edward Trent, but he had laid a small card beside her hand and held it in place with her rosary.

The nun had no intention of contacting the professor again, and she scolded herself for confiding in a man she had only known for a brief moment of time.

She pushed the card into the depth of her pocket and erased Edward Trent from her thoughts.

XIII

It was the third day that Orla hadn't left her room, her bed in fact, since the funeral. Sister Ophelia despaired.

Mother Superior had afforded her seven days leave and in that time the nun was hoping to return to the convent safe in the knowledge her sibling was coping in the aftermath of the tragedy. Sadly, that was not yet the case.

"I've brought you some tea and a slice of cake," declared the nun entering her sister's bedroom.

She drew back the drapes, washing the room with sunlight.

"It's such a beautiful day. I thought we might take a walk, get some fresh air?"

Orla didn't reply, nor did she move from the ball shaped impression she made beneath the duvet.

"It's ginger cake… your favourite."

There was slight movement as an arm shot out from beneath the blankets and Orla turned onto her back. She stared into space, unblinking.

"It was Amelia's favourite too," mumbled Orla as she trembled beneath the covers.

She looked pale, eyes red and swollen, and was still wearing her black dress from the funeral.

"Why don't you take a shower, freshen up?" suggested the nun. The air in the room was pungent, heavy beneath the remnants of stale perspiration.

Sister Ophelia was about to leave the room when Orla revealed, "I saw her last night."

The nun returned to her sister's bedside. "Saw who?"

"Amelia, she was here last night, standing beside my bed."

"You dreamed of her?"

"Not a dream!" snapped Orla, "standing right there on the spot where you are now. Her eyes were black as the night sky, staring. She didn't look like Amelia, but I knew it was her. A mother knows her own child."

Sister Ophelia nodded as a shiver coasted her spine, Orla's words recounting the chilling memory of Sister Irene's missing eyes, and the gaping bloodied holes that stared back.

"She was dirty," continued Orla, "muddy, soiled from head to toe, like she'd crawled out of her grave. Her burial dress in tatters, her feet bare as the day she was born."

The nun tried desperately to change the subject, but Orla continued, "she blames me for what happened! For allowing such evil into our home."

She was referring to Flora now.

"You were dreaming," protested the nun, "a grieving mind playing tricks in the darkness."

Orla violently threw aside the duvet, "so this is a dream?" she hissed.

The nun felt the impact of a punch to the stomach, winding her instantly as she stepped closer to the bed.

There on the crispness of the bedsheet two muddy handprints rested, child sized and undeniable.

Orla began to laugh maniacally.

Sister Ophelia felt for the security of her rosary, gripping it tightly as she recited the Lord's Prayer.

Orla grew agitated, crouching like an animal upon the bed. The nun continued to pray, thrusting forward the cross that dangled amongst the wooden beads of her rosary. An ungodly presence had possessed her sister.

Orla's face twisted, eyes growing wider, teeth bared as she levitated above the sheets.

"Your God can't help you now!" snarled a voice from the depth of Orla's floating body. The voice was not her own. A guttural baritone spoke the words as Orla mouthed them, writhing and spitting as she did so.

The nun's prayers grew louder and more forceful as she dangled the rosary from her hand. The image of the cross swayed pendulously before the creature, the ultimate icon against evil.

Orla screamed as she sank onto the bed. A mirror shattered to the ground on the other side of the room and the windows flew open, allowing a blast of cold air to invade the room, retreating just as quickly. The evil had left her. The room was silent.

Sister Ophelia's hands were trembling as she covered the stillness of her sister's body, then hurried to secure the windows.

Orla was peaceful now. Colour had returned to her cheeks and she was breathing calmly.

Downstairs, the nun raced to the glass cabinet and poured a large whiskey, hoping to calm her nerves before returning to Orla's side.

She wasn't sure what she had witnessed, perhaps her first encounter with a demon. Orla was clearly the target, but the message was aimed directly towards her.

The nun gathered herself together. With rosary in one hand and Bible in the other, she headed cautiously back to the bedroom.

To her relief, Orla was sleeping soundly. The nun placed the Bible on her nightstand and fastened a silver cross around her neck. She made a call to the convent and asked to speak with Father Ignatius, but the priest was inebriated and had passed out in his study.

At dinnertime, Orla made a surprising visit to the kitchen, unnerving Sister Ophelia with her sudden presence.

"How are you feeling?" asked the nun apprehensively, as Orla crossed the room.

"I'm fine," came the reply, as Orla took a seat at the table. They dined together and shared a bottle of wine.

Orla appeared to have no recollection of the events of earlier and, for the first time since Amelia's death, seemed brighter. She chattered incessantly about everything except her dead daughter or the visitations she had encountered.

That night, Sister Ophelia made her way to bed. She prayed as usual before sitting to read a passage from her Bible. Orla had retired slightly earlier, enveloping her sister in a tight embrace and whispering, "thank you," as she left the room.

A sudden creak on the landing caught the nun's attention. She glanced towards the crack beneath her door as a shadow passed in the glow of her night light. It faltered momentarily as Sister Ophelia held her breath. The sight of small, dirty toenails appeared beneath the gap.

The nun dare not move, hugging her Bible tightly, watching anxiously as her heart thumped within her chest. It seemed an age before the toes disappeared, along with the shadow as it moved along the corridor. The nun exhaled loudly, her breath trembling with fear.

Sister Ophelia pushed the duvet aside and crept slowly towards the door. Placing a shaky hand upon it she opened it cautiously. The door opened to nothing but darkness except for the dim sliver of lamplight that lit the patch of carpet in front of her. The nun stepped forward, hitting the coldness of something wet beneath her feet. Muddy footprints decorated the ground where she stood. Small child sized footprints. She followed them cautiously as they lead her towards Orla's room and disappeared.

The nun leant against the painted panelling and listened carefully. She could hear the faint mumbling of her sister's voice inside. Was she talking in her sleep? Perhaps dreaming?

Sister Ophelia knew deep inside that neither was the answer.

The nun nervously turned the handle, opening the door with trepidation.

A blast of freezing air escaped, as if all the windows of the house were open and it was the middle of winter. She shivered beneath the blanket of cold and called to Orla. There was no reply. She had to face the darkness, though it overpowered her imagination. Feeling for the light switch, she stepped forward, but light evaded her. Only darkness invited her inside.

Sister Ophelia swung her rosary like a guiding weapon as she called her sister's name.

Orla didn't answer.

The nun stepped further into the room. Her eyes adjusting slowly to the void of blackness.

She sensed a presence in the distance. The stench of it soured the air as she retched momentarily.

In the shadow of the bedroom, she traced the outline of Orla sitting upright on the bed, mumbling incoherently. She wasn't alone. Standing beside her was a figure. It manifested as that of a small child, Amelia perhaps, yet Sister Ophelia knew its façade masked a far more sinister occupant. Its eyes pierced the darkness with a red glow, staring, unblinking.

As a solitary finger of moonlight touched it, the figure dissolved, and the room sprang to life with returning electricity.

Orla had lain back on her pillows now, eyes closed as though nothing untoward had taken place.

Sister Ophelia closed the door and hurried to her room, locking the door behind her. She climbed into bed and slept with her rosary firmly bound around her hand. She blessed herself and prayed for guidance as she struggled to find comfort in sleep.

The light of a new day can convince the memory that events of the night before were nothing but a bad dream. The seeds of doubt are sown as the mind chooses not to believe and labels the occurrence, 'unexplained', but as the nun pushed back the duvet, she witnessed the smear of dried mud clinging to the bedsheet. In that moment, she knew that everything she thought she'd witnessed was actually real.

That morning, Orla had risen early and busied herself with breakfast.

"Pancakes or bacon butties?" she asked as the nun entered the kitchen.

Sister Ophelia was surprised to find her sister's mood so vibrant.

"Now that's a difficult choice," replied Sister Ophelia with a smile. "How about pancakes and bacon butties?"

Orla seemed not to mind the extra work, humming to herself as she beavered at the stove.

"What's that tune?" questioned the nun, certain that she knew it but couldn't place it.

Orla didn't answer.

As they dined on breakfast, Sister Ophelia felt compelled to mention the event of the night before.

"Were you having a bad dream last night?" she queried.

Orla answered without hesitation, "not bad at all, in fact the best dream I could have had."

"How so?" enquired the nun.

"I dreamt Amelia visited me. She told me not to worry, that I would be with her again soon. I felt comforted by her words and safe knowing that we would be reunited," replied Orla with a wide smile.

Sister Ophelia had to question whether the person sitting opposite her was, in fact, her sister.

Her outward appearance was as expected, but the nun knew that the woman sitting opposite her at the table was notably different. It was almost as if her personality had transformed overnight. In truth, it was unsettling. The predictable, sensitive Orla seemed to have discovered a whole new concept for coping with grief.

She hummed the same tune sporadically, smiled and danced around the kitchen as though her period of mourning Amelia had ended.

After breakfast, Orla disappeared into the lounge. Music was suddenly playing, blasting from her old gramophone.

Sister Ophelia recognised it as the tune her sibling had been humming.

In the living room, Orla had poured herself a large glass of wine and was attempting to swallow it at speed.

"Orla!" shouted the nun, crossing the room to adjust the volume.

"Hey, what are you doing?" cried Orla as the music mellowed.

"You'll have the neighbours complaining," explained Sister Ophelia.

"Let them!" came the reply as she headed towards the volume button.

"Since when did you drink wine at 9.30 in the morning?" queried the nun, knowing that her sister was nothing more than a social, just-a-small-one-for-me drinker.

"Since I'm celebrating," replied Orla sarcastically.

The music was bellowing again.

The empty sleeve of 'Highway to Hell' lay discarded on the floor. It was a record their father had played when they were children. His favourite band, AC/DC, accredited for the tune.

Orla crossed the room with exuberant dance moves, turning the music up even louder.

Sister Ophelia rushed to intervene, but before she could reach the volume button, Orla pushed her forcefully aside. The nun hit the sofa with a thud and crumpled to the ground, shocked by her sister's strength.

Orla turned towards her, eyes black as night, a smile as wide as her lips would allow. She smashed the wineglass against the wall and pulled the serrated stem across her throat.

Sister Ophelia cried out as Orla hit the ground, blood pooling instantly, gushing from the depth of her severed neck. Orla choked and spluttered as blood flooded her lungs. Her life faded rapidly away.

By the time paramedics arrived, Orla had been reunited with her daughter.

XIV

In the aftermath of her sister's death, Ophelia returned to the convent perturbed by what she had witnessed.

Was faith failing her? Had she allowed doubt to embrace her belief? She prayed in the chapel for several hours, hoping to receive the answer. As she rose from the harshness of the stone floor, something floated to the ground beside her. A piece of paper had dislodged itself from the crease of a fold in her habit.

It was the card that Edward Trent had deposited beside her on the sofa that evening a week ago.

The nun felt the sudden warmth of divine inspiration wash over her. Perhaps this man was the answer to her prayer.

In the solitude of her room, Sister Ophelia wrote a short note to the professor and prayed for a swift reply.

A couple of days later, Sister Grace handed her a small white envelope. Sure enough, Edward had answered her plea:

> *Dear Sister Ophelia,*
>
> *I was disturbed to learn of your sister's untimely death and the circumstances you describe. I am uncertain how I can help, but I suggest we meet in the university library, Friday evening at 7pm.*
>
> *I do so hope to see you there.*
>
> *Regards,*
> *Edward*

As the nuns dispersed from Vespers, Sister Ophelia caught the attention of Sister Grace.

"I do so need your help, Sister, with a little matter on Friday evening," declared the nun.

"And you shall have it," replied Sister Grace, who could always be relied upon for her discretion.

"Following Vespers, I shall need to leave the convent for a short time. If anyone were to ask of my whereabouts, tell them I retired early with a migraine and wished to be left alone."

Sister Grace nodded enthusiastically, "of course Sister."

Friday arrived, and all day, Sister Ophelia's stomach struggled and squirmed with painful spasms. As Vespers ended, she fashioned the shape of a make believe body in her bed and left the convent beneath the veil of dusk.

Her destination was fortunately within walking distance as she hurried along the dimly lit lane that lead to the outskirts of town.

The university claimed a large portion of land which almost encroached upon the gardens of the convent, their division marked only by a crumbling stone wall. The vast campus sprawled across a wide area of town. It was an incredible landmark boasting multiple turrets, a round tower, and extensive carved architecture. It was an imposing building, built around the same time as the convent, with centuries of history hidden within its walls.

Sister Ophelia slipped inside the building via the back entrance and followed directions to the library.

A creaking door swiftly followed by the musk of bibliosmia told the nun she was in the right place. She entered cautiously, anxiously searching for Edward Trent.

"Sister!" his voice bellowed above her. She looked up to find the professor standing on the first floor landing of the library.

He smiled as he ascended the stairs towards her, holding a couple of ancient looking books in his hands.

"So pleased you could make it," he began.

"Sadly, I haven't much time," interrupted Sister Ophelia, slightly perturbed by her act of deceit.

Edward placed the books on the nearest desk and took a seat on the edge.

"Your letter was most enlightening, Sister. I assume from our last conversation at your niece's funeral that this has something to do with the child you mentioned."

Sister Ophelia thought for a moment. In the pandemonium of grief, she had failed to think about Flora. It seemed obvious now though, the untimely deaths and the presence of Flora were no coincidence.

"Did you locate the child?" asked the professor interrupting her thoughts.

The nun shook her head as snippets of their previous discussion gnawed at her memory. That evening, she had revealed more information to Edward Trent than she had intended. Had she mentioned the child's name? The answer evaded her, as did much of their conversation. As far as she could recall, she had talked about Flora in a hypothetical sense only.

"Sister, are you all right?"

The nun dragged herself back into the moment and smiled.

"What do you know of her parents?" enquired the professor.

"Absolutely nothing," she replied, "other than she was born at the convent a couple of years before my arrival."

"An unmarried mother," declared Edward knowingly, "then there must be a record of her birth and, as such, her parents."

"Perhaps, but that part of the convent closed down shortly after I arrived. Where the records are now, I have no idea."

"It is imperative that you locate them, Sister," commanded Edward.

The nun glanced at him, slightly bewildered.

"I am certain that the answer to understanding this child will begin with her parents," comforted the professor.

"I don't quite follow Mr Trent. What do you mean by understanding?" queried the nun.

"Come now, Sister, we both know we are not dealing with an ordinary child. Isn't that the reason you contacted me?"

Sister Ophelia paused for thought.

"I suppose it was, but not primarily. I hoped you could shed some light on the events at my sister's home," explained the nun, "offer a rational explanation for what happened."

Edward shook his head, "I'm afraid rational explanations are seldom the answer in my profession. In this case, what you are looking for lies within the child."

The nun knew he was right, though she hated to admit it. If Flora's ability was so strong as a child, what would she be capable of in years to come, as an adult?

Sister Ophelia felt pained as she wrestled with the vision of Flora's innocent face and the possibility of something sinister growing inside her. She could not deny witnessing the aftermath of Flora's ability, both at the convent and in her sister's home. She rose from her seat and paced the library's polished oak.

"She's just an innocent child," she murmured, gripping the skirt of her habit with tightened fists.

Edward Trent crossed to a water machine and retrieved a cup of refreshment for his guest.

"Here, Sister, please sit down," he soothed.

Sister Ophelia obeyed. Her head swimming with questions.

"The child you describe has something inside her that makes her different from other children, correct?"

The nun nodded. "Yes, a gift!"

Edward frowned at her words.

"You don't believe she has a gift?" demanded the nun.

"On the contrary, I wholehearted believe the child has a power that cannot be explained. I merely question your description."

"Alright, a power then, if you prefer," accepted the nun.

Edward Trent sighed deeply and rose from the desk.

"And where do you think this power comes from?"

Sister Ophelia sighed. She wanted the answer to be God, but she could not bring herself to say it.

"You don't believe it's God given, do you?" queried the professor.

The nun searched for a fitting reply. Sadly, it evaded her.

"I believe she was born with an innate… power! Whether God is responsible, I cannot say with certainty," she replied with frustration.

Edward paused before answering. He searched for a reply that would not desecrate the nun's religious conviction.

"Sister, not every miracle is the work of God. Thessalonians chapter 2, verse 8-9 reminds us that 'Satan has the power to perform counterfeit miracles,'" recited the professor.

"I know my Bible, Mr Trent," groaned Sister Ophelia with an air of contempt. "She is merely a child. How can she know of anything but innocence? And yet you use her name in the same sentence as that of Satan!"

"Children are innocent until they reach the biblical age of accountability," replied the professor, realising that he had failed in his quest not to upset the nun.

"Accountability? The child is only seven," hailed Sister Ophelia.

"Then she will shortly be deemed accountable for her actions," replied Edward.

Sister Ophelia shook her head. "You're implying that Flora's gift is the work of the Devil and that she is aware of her actions?"

"I'm offering it as a counter explanation," began Edward, "think about it. Every so-called 'miracle' she has performed is followed closely by tragedy and death."

Sister Ophelia struggled with the professor's words. He was challenging everything she believed. She was desperate for answers, but all Edward had given her so far were quotes from the Bible. She hated to admit it, but he did make a good argument.

"You do believe in the Devil, don't you, Sister?"

"Of course," came the reply, "but I refuse to believe that it could possibly exist in a sweet little child." Sister Ophelia spoke the words with a heavy cloud of doubt raining over them.

Edward shook his head, "in no way do I wish to discredit your faith, Sister, but you must heed my words not only for the sake of the child, but for the sake of every life she touches."

Was it possible for the Devil to live in someone so sweet, so innocent? If it was, and it was a pretty big 'if' in the nun's opinion, then the child had no consensual understanding of it. She was merely used as an unconscious vessel to orchestrate its desire. Flora could not, as Edward implied, be aware of her dark side.

The professor, recognising the nun's struggle by her expression, pushed the books he had retrieved earlier towards her. They were invaluable at answering awkward, sometimes inexplicable questions.

"Read these. You may just find the answers to your questions. In the meantime, find out all you can about the parents," he soothed, leaving the nun to her thoughts and disappearing from sight.

Sister Ophelia hurried back to the convent, conscious of the hour and the possibility of Mother Superior's scrutiny.

Fortunately, she made it back to her bedroom without complication.

She hid the professor's books beneath her mattress and climbed into bed.

XV

Flora was ready for school. She was excited for her first day sitting between Rita and Alexis on the back seat of Mr Moreton's car.

"I think you'll be in my class," enthused Rita, "you will love the teacher. She's really kind and helpful."

Flora smiled. It was exciting to feel part of a family again, even though this one was huge compared to her time spent with Orla and Amelia.

The school was much bigger than the convent, modern and spacious.

The classroom was already buzzing with life. Girls chatting eagerly, boys throwing rubbish at each other, and the teacher, a tall, slender, grey-haired woman was writing instructions on the board.

"Miss Templeton, this is Flora," announced Rita proudly.

The woman stopped writing immediately and stooped to welcome her new pupil. "I'm so happy that you are joining us, Flora. Pick an empty seat and class will begin shortly," she advised.

Rita took Flora's hand and lead her towards the back of the classroom, where she pointed out her own desk and suggested Flora take the one next to it.

The morning went quickly, and suddenly lunchtime was upon them.

In the school canteen, Flora queued to survey the array of gourmet delights available, then joined Rita on a table with several other girls.

"Who are you?" growled a chubby girl with no front teeth and oversized spectacles.

"Don't be so rude Fiona, this is Flora," replied Rita, "she's with me, so move up and make room."

Flora slotted into the group with keen eyes surveying her from every direction. It was an uncomfortable lunchtime experience fraught with questions, observations, and unwanted attention.

"Pay no mind to Fiona, she can be awfully bullish with new girls, but once she gets to know you, she'll be fine," comforted Rita.

"It's okay," smiled Flora, "she doesn't scare me."

It was a bold statement for one so meek and mild as Flora. After all, her petite frame and small stature were no physical match for the height and build of Fiona McPherson, but Flora felt invincible, confident, even mildly confrontational.

Rita had noticed a change in her new friend, too. The timid, shy girl who had first entered her bedroom had grown in confidence. There was an expression on her face and a glint in her eye that hadn't been there before.

If Rita were meeting her for the first time, Flora would make her feel uneasy, intimidated, almost afraid.

Sister Ophelia had found it difficult to concentrate on her duties that morning. Her thoughts were constantly kidnapped by the books that lay beneath her mattress. She served lunch as normal, then hurried in the direction of her room for a moment of quiet reflection.

Instead of using the time to pray, she felt for the books and tossed them onto the bed. The first was titled 'The Innocence of Evil'. It portrayed firsthand accounts of demonic possession of children, explaining how an entity deviously and maliciously inhabited the child's soul. There were thousands of references to case studies around the world, each one similar to the next. Photo images of young, vulnerable boys and girls were disturbing. Children like Flora suckling at the breast of Satan. The outcome seemed as grim as the beginning, with only a small percentage clinging to life after exorcism.

The nun closed the book. The bell was ringing for Vespers. She had spent the entire afternoon immersed in a book about the Devil. How would she explain that to Mother Superior if her absence within the convent had been noted?

Fortunately, the Reverend Mother seemed preoccupied. She had spent her time entertaining a bishop directly from the holy city itself. The nun almost collided with them as they departed the office and headed toward the chapel.

Without a second thought, Sister Ophelia seized the opportunity and entered the empty room.

In a far corner, Father Ignatius lay slumped in a drunken coma, sleeping off the effects of an empty brandy bottle.

The nun paid no mind to him and hurried towards the filing cabinets standing in line behind the holy mother's desk. At that moment, as she surveyed the alphabetical system, she realised she had no idea of Flora's surname.

Nevertheless, that wasn't going to stop her. She flicked through the files with ease, stopping when Flora's name appeared.

The contents of the folder were scanty, holding merely a birth certificate and a sealed envelope. The certificate itself was as sparse of information as the file, stating Christian T as her father and Marley Sutton as her mother. The child's name simply read FLORA. The registrar's name was almost indecipherable, but seemed to read 'Baloid'.

The nun committed the names to memory and replaced the file. Father Ignatius was stirring as she headed for the door.

"Sister, is there something I can help you with?" he mumbled with a slur in his tone.

"Nothing, Father, thank you," began the nun. Then she stopped and turned back towards him.

"I wondered if we had heard of the child, Flora, and how she was getting on in the outside world?" quizzed the nun unashamedly.

Father Ignatius righted his posture and reached for the empty brandy glass beside him. He raised it to his lips before realising it was devoid of liquid.

"That's a question for the Reverend Mother," he answered, "though I'm certain she is still living with a family in County Bottega."

"That's very reassuring, Father. She's being fostered there?"

"I expect so, Sister, a charitable family of God no doubt," proffered the priest.

Sister Ophelia wanted to pick the old man's brains further, but she knew that doing so would seem inappropriate, and she didn't want to arouse suspicion with her multitude of questions.

Father Ignatius pulled himself to a standing position and staggered towards the cabinet beside the window. It housed his stash of alcohol, though it had recently been raided by Mother Superior and was empty of contents.

The nun couldn't help but query the cause of the priest's insatiable addiction. She remembered it being mentioned that Father Ignatius had once worked as an exorcist for the Vatican. Perhaps it was an experience in that role that was responsible.

"Father! What do you know of exorcism?" she asked.

The old priest suddenly stumbled, the effect of inebriation or the directness of the nun's question causing his unsteadiness.

He grasped her hand to gain his balance, his eyes wide, his face the colour of his white collar.

"That's a word that has no place in my vocabulary," he stuttered, reaching for the safety of his chair.

"I didn't mean to upset you Father, I am merely questioning its purpose and validity."

The priest's body trembled as he uttered a reply.

"It's a practice that, in my opinion, should be banned, Sister. No good ever comes from challenging the Devil. Victory is rare in a battle such as that."

Father Ignatius buried his head in his hands and rocked from side to side.

"Then how are we to banish evil from the souls of innocents?" demanded the nun. "How do we save the afflicted?"

The priest, without changing his posture, replied, "we don't, Sister. We leave them to their fate. Only God can save them if he sees fit."

They were harsh words from a man of the cloth.

Sister Ophelia feared she could not push the priest any further. He was already on the brink of breaking point.

"How was school?" enquired Mrs M as the children returned home.

"It was fine," replied Amrita.

"Flora, how did you find it?" asked the foster mother, noting the child had not offered an answer.

"A bit scary, but nothing that I can't handle," replied the girl with an angelic smile.

Mrs M laughed, "wash up now. Dinner is almost ready."

That night, whilst the family slept, Flora crept from her bed and entered the kitchen. She removed a small knife from the cutlery drawer and hid it in her school bag.

"Where've you been?" whispered Rita on her return.

"Just getting a drink of water," replied Flora. "Good night!"

XVI

The following day, Sister Ophelia took a walk into town to visit the university library again. Hoping to avoid Edward Trent and his sanctimonious sermons.

The library was buzzing with students, and thankfully no sign of the professor.

"Can I help you, Sister?" asked a freckly faced young man at the reception desk.

"I hope you can," replied the nun with a smile. "I'm looking for records of foster carers and a register of births for the last decade."

"Right this way," directed the young man, pausing beside a machine the nun had never encountered before.

"I'll get you the microfiche," he stated and disappeared.

Sister Ophelia sat before the contraption and looked it up and down. She searched for a button to turn it on, mumbling to herself and scolding her ignorance.

"Need a hand, Sister?"

The young man had returned.

"What makes you think that?" chuckled the nun.

"Just the way you're looking at it."

"I'm trying to work out how to turn it on."

The young man offered a quick lesson, which she was grateful for. A typewriter was the closest she'd ever come to such a machine, and that was many years ago.

"Thank you, that's so kind," stated Sister Ophelia.

"Call me if you get stuck. I'm Donal."

Sister Ophelia flicked awkwardly through the microfiche in search of Flora's birth certificate. It heralded the same information she had already seen and nothing more.

Perhaps finding a foster family in County Bottega would be easier, but it wasn't.

The nun caught Donal's eye.

"What exactly are you looking for, Sister?" he asked.

The nun explained she was trying to trace a foster family, but wasn't having much luck.

"Have you any other information other than just names?" queried Donal as he took a seat beside her.

The nun shook her head. "Not really."

"Well, to start with fostering is easy," explained the young man. "It'll be child welfare services that you'll be needing. That's the number to call," pointed Donal.

Sister Ophelia clasped her hands together with excitement. Donal was heaven sent.

"If you follow me into the back office, you'll be able to use the phone," he offered.

Donal dialled the number. "Here you can speak to someone who might be able to help," he advised.

"Good morning. How can I be of help?" asked a cheery voice.

"Good morning. My name is Sister Ophelia from St. Catharine's Convent. I'm trying to trace a little girl called Flora. She was resident with us from birth and I'm just enquiring after her wellbeing."

For a moment, the line went silent as though the woman at the other end had disappeared.

"Hello!" pleaded the nun, hoping for a reply.

"Yes, sorry about that, interference, it happens a lot," explained the woman, "now, Flora, you said, didn't you?"

Sister Ophelia crossed her fingers, a pagan symbol she rarely used, but on this occasion, she felt the need for a little extra help.

"The only Flora I have is Flora Sutton. She's living with the Moreton family in County Bottega. A lovely family with many years' experience in the fostering game."

The words came as a relief. Not only had she found Flora's whereabouts, but her previously unrecorded surname, which unusually was the same as her mother's.

"How can I find the Moreton's?" enquired Sister Ophelia. "I would love to see Flora again."

"I'm sorry, but that information is classified. I'm unable to give out their address," came the reply.

The nun was disappointed, but thanked the woman anyway.

"No luck?" quizzed Donal.

"The child I'm searching for is living with a family called the Moreton's, but their address is classified," sighed Sister Ophelia, handing back the phone.

"The Moreton's," repeated Donal, "I can help with that, Sister," grinned the young man, "I went to school with their son Adam, I know exactly where they live."

Donal scribbled down the address, and Sister Ophelia placed it in her pocket.

"Now I just need to find the child's mother, Marley Sutton,"

Donal pulled out a telephone book and scrolled through the list of surnames beginning with the letter 'S'

Donal groaned.

"What's wrong?" asked the nun.

"There are so many Suttons, it would take you an age to contact each of these," he declared. "What else do you know about Marley Sutton?"

Sister Ophelia thought for a moment, but the answer didn't reveal itself.

"What about her date of birth?" he quizzed.

There was a silent pause as the nun disappeared into thought.

"Her age is on her child's birth certificate," she declared triumphantly. "Would that be of any use?"

Donal nodded as he returned to the microfiche.

Flora's birth certificate heralded her mother's date of birth. Donal loaded the microfiche for 1954 and scrolled carefully.

"Here she is," he declared excitedly. "She was born in Ballykilne. That's a village on the other side of the island."

"Then that's where I need to go," thanked the nun.

If it hadn't been inappropriate, Sister Ophelia would have hugged and kissed the young man who had helped her. Instead, she blessed him and headed back towards the convent.

That night, Sister Ophelia opened up the second book that Edward Trent had given her, 'Hunting Evil' written by none other than the professor himself. It was an absorbing explanation of the signs and symptoms of the mortally possessed, how to recognise them and how to deal with their evil inhabitants. Of course, it wasn't that simple. There were so many malevolent entities that first they had to be identified, their presence confirmed, and finally, they had to be challenged. It was a courageous fight between good and evil and usually ended by one of more of the participants losing their life. In all, it made for gruesome reading, with little in the way of comfort.

Sister Ophelia penned a letter to Professor Trent, declaring her success in locating one of Flora's parents. She kept the detail to a minimum for fear Edward might decide to take matters into his own hands.

She wanted to find Marley Sutton and visit Flora before meeting with the professor for a second time.

Sister Grace, who was on shopping duty, agreed to mail the letter on her way to the supermarket.

XVIII

Flora was up early the next morning and helped to prepare breakfast for the other children.

She sang on the way to school and skipped through the corridors to class.

"What's she so happy about?" asked Alexis, but Amrita had no idea.

"Just enjoying school, I guess," she shrugged.

"Odd child," replied Alexis sarcastically.

At lunchtime, Flora tucked herself in next to Fiona McPherson, who pretended to ignore her the whole time.

When Fiona was deep in conversation with the girl next to her, Flora removed the kitchen knife from her schoolbag and dropped into the front pocket of Fiona's rucksack.

In the first lesson after lunch, biology, Fiona pulled out her crisp, white apron in readiness to dissect a pig's heart. As she did so, something solid hit the floor beside her feet.

The teacher, with her acute bat-like hearing, turned to witness the silver blade of a kitchen knife sitting on the laboratory floor.

"Fiona McPherson, what on earth are you doing with a knife in school?" she growled.

Fiona tried many times to protest her innocence, but to no avail. When the boy standing behind her confirmed the object had fallen from Fiona's bag, she was ordered to the headteacher's office immediately.

Everyone stared in shock. That is, everyone except for Flora, who was busy reading the instruction manual on the pig heart dissection.

By home time, news of Fiona's dangerous item was common knowledge, as was the fact that her parents had been called to school and she had been expelled for an entire week.

Flora smiled inwardly. She would enjoy Fiona's absence.

Rita sensed that Flora was somehow involved in Fiona's expulsion from school, though she couldn't prove it. It was just a feeling.

Edward Trent didn't send a response for almost two weeks. He'd been abroad on a last minute short secondment.

He wanted to meet in the library again the following evening.

Sister Ophelia slipped away from the convent once again beneath the veil of darkness and found the professor waiting for her.

"You read them?" he queried as she handed back the books.

"I have," replied the nun.

"Your thoughts?"

"Much as before," replied Sister Ophelia. "I acknowledge there is evil in the world and it comes in many forms, but I still can't see it living inside the child."

"You read about the other children, just as angelic looking and innocent?" he questioned.

"I did, and the evidence is compelling. I don't doubt that it happens to some children, but not to her."

"The innocent, beguiling smile, the blue eyes are nothing but a mask, Sister. A wolf in sheep's clothing!" quoted the professor.

Edward Trent sighed heavily and slumped into the chair beside the nun.

"Think about it rationally, Sister," he pleaded, "every inexplicable incident has involved this child. The nun at the convent suddenly given life, when you knew she was dead, hung by the neck. Then your niece Amelia savaged by her own dog. The dog that the child had given life to." Edward was desperately animated now, his hands flying in every direction as he struggled to convince the nun sitting before him, "and Orla, your sister, taking her own life in front of you after declaring that she had been visited by her dead daughter the night before."

"Orla and Sister Irene were suicides. I don't think the child can be blamed for that," replied the nun, "and Amelia, the actions of a mad, rabid dog."

"You don't really believe that, do you?" demanded Edward, rising from his chair and pacing the floor. "What more must I do for you to believe me, Sister? The child is the catalyst. We must find her before she harms anyone else."

Sister Ophelia clutched at the note in her pocket. She wasn't sure she wanted to share the child's whereabouts with Edward Trent. She wasn't sure what he intended to do.

"And if we find her, what then?" she asked.

"I don't want to hurt the child, Sister. I merely want to help her," replied the professor with conviction.

"And if we find the child, how will you help her?"

"By exorcism, of course. It is a known practice in your own faith. A professional, experienced exorcist is what she needs."

"Well, I'm afraid I don't know where she is, other than she's living with a foster family, but that's all the information I was afforded."

Edward stared into her eyes. She held his gaze confidently, hoping to dispel any doubts he might have. After all, she was married to God and not in the habit of lying, maybe just a little bending of the truth.

"Very well," accepted Edward, "but the parents, you have their details?"

Sister Ophelia felt happier to release that information, as there was so little of it. Edward wrote down the names and scratched the tip of his nose with the end of his pen, "curious that there is no surname for the father, I would have thought it obligatory."

"I thought that too," agreed the nun. "I suppose our only hope of contacting the parents lies with the mother, Marley Sutton."

"I have to leave for India in the morning," stated the professor. "I trust I can leave this with you?"

The air felt clearer as Professor Trent left the room. Sister Ophelia sighed loudly, releasing the tension that had built up inside her during what felt like a pressured interrogation.

Edward meant well, she was sure of it, but in his eyes Flora had already been tried and found guilty. She had to know that Edward Trent was correct before allowing him anywhere near her.

XVIII

A couple of days later, Mother Superior left the convent for a trip to Vatican City. No one knew the purpose of her visit, but she was beyond excited.

Sister Ophelia intended to take full advantage of the Holy Mother's absence.

County Bottega sat fifteen miles southeast of the convent. Sister Ophelia hurried into town and hailed a taxi. Sister Grace had kindly agreed to cover her kitchen duties while she was gone and fend off inquisitive questions from the other nuns.

County Bottega sat in the midst of lush, green countryside with a small pebbly beach just yards from its centre.

The house was called Ballymorton and sat at the far end of Castle Road.

It was a terraced home with a small front garden and a white picket fence. The sound of children could be heard as Sister Ophelia exited the taxi.

It took a couple of loud knocks for the nun to be heard, then the door opened to reveal a plump, red-haired boy, who promptly bowed at her presence.

"Who is it, Rory?" shouted a woman's voice from inside.

"It's Jesus' wife," replied Rory, with a broad smile.

Momentarily, a red-faced lady appeared at his side.

"Oh my goodness, Rory, where are your manners? Please do come in Sister."

The interior of the house was small, but cosy and might have looked bigger had it not been so untidy and brimming with clutter and ornaments. Nevertheless, it had a warm and welcoming atmosphere.

Almost instantly, as the nun took a seat on the sofa, a group of nosey children filled the space around her. The boys bowing and the girls curtsying as though they were meeting royalty.

Sister Ophelia scanned the row of eager faces in front of her, searching for Flora. Then, between the push and shove of elbows and shoulders, she spied the little girl's blue eyes twinkling amidst the crowd.

"Flora!" declared the nun, opening her arms wide.

Flora pushed through the wall of children and embraced the nun eagerly.

There was warmth in the little girl's touch. How could that be if she were governed by evil, as the professor suggested?

"How are you?" queried Sister Ophelia.

"I'm very good, thank you," replied the child.

"Oh, she's a peach," added Mrs M, sending the group scattering with a clap of her hands.

"I was so worried about you," proffered the nun.

"How's Daphne?" questioned Flora.

"Daphne is just fine. She misses you, of course. We all do!"

"Except the Reverend Mother," declared Flora.

The nun shook her head and hugged Flora some more.

Mrs M brought tea and biscuits for Sister Ophelia and Flora to enjoy.

"Have you brought news of a family, Sister?" queried Mrs M. "Is that why you're here?"

Sister Ophelia felt a sudden flush of guilt burn her cheeks.

"No, no family yet, but hopefully one day," she comforted, watching Flora's smile fade.

"Am I coming back to the convent with you?" proposed the little girl.

Sister Ophelia took hold of her hand. "And why would you want to do that when you have such a lovely home here?" she teased.

Flora whispered, "to kill the Mother Superior!"

For a moment the nun paused as if time itself had stopped. Had she heard the child correctly? Did she say what she thought she had?

Flora was giggling beside her and Mrs M was sipping at her teacup, apparently unaware of the comment.

Sister Ophelia was overcome with doubt. Suddenly her hand trembled and the teacup she was holding tumbled to the floor, spilling its contents into the depth of the carpets fibres.

"I'm so sorry," she apologised, panic-stricken.

"No bother, Sister, it'll clean."

Mrs M, unperturbed by the accident, sent Flora into the kitchen for a damp cloth.

"There's accidents like this every day, Sister, with so many clumsy children running around," explained the foster mother.

For some reason, Flora never returned from the kitchen, even though the nun waited for another half hour.

"Where has she got to?" chuckled Mrs M, "no doubt back upstairs playing and forgotten all about the cloth and you, Sister."

The nun, feeling slightly uneasy, called time on her visit and thanked Mrs M for her hospitality.

As they approached the front door, Sister Ophelia asked, "have there been any problems with Flora at all?"

"What kind of problems?" replied Mrs M.

Sister Ophelia brushed off the question with, "just checking that she's settled at school?"

"Oh, she's adorable, settled like a professional. Got lots of friends and the teachers say she's achieving well above her required age level."

"That's comforting to hear," replied the nun.

At the bottom of the path, Sister Ophelia stopped before the gate. She turned her gaze back towards the house and searched its windows. From the top right window, Flora was watching her. Her expression was stern as she pressed her face against the glass.

She held the nun in a trance-like gaze. Then, suddenly, she broke a smile and waved enthusiastically as Sister Ophelia headed towards the town centre to find a taxi home.

XIX

The day before Mother Superior was due to return from Rome, Daphne went missing.

The nuns scoured the convent, the outbuildings, the garden, the graveyard, and the surrounding area in search of her.

It was Agnes who submitted that Daphne was most probably in the dungeon.

"Why would she go there?" queried Sister Grace.

"She likes it down there," came the reply.

"Really, Agnes? She has nothing but unhappy memories of the dungeon and the hole in the wall. Daphne seems to have frequented it far more than any other child recently," declared Sister Maread, who was a relatively new postulant.

"She has a friend down there," added Agnes, who shared a dormitory and the bed next to Daphne's.

The nuns glanced at each other questioningly.

"Stop it, Agnes, you're telling lies," growled an overly flustered Sister Grace. "There'll be no supper for you if you keep it up!"

Agnes bowed her head and said nothing more.

"The only friend she can have down there is a rat," boasted Sister Maread, rolling her eyes.

"I'll go and check it out," offered Sister Ophelia, who rescued a torch from the hall closet and headed in the direction of the dungeon.

Fiona McPherson returned to school a day earlier than she was supposed to. She found Flora occupying her usual seat in the classroom.

"That's my seat," growled Fiona, throwing her bag down on the desk.

"Not anymore, it's not!" came the reply.

"What did you say?" queried Fiona, stepping closer to Flora's side.

"I said not anymore, it's not. Are you deaf as well as stupid?" growled Flora.

Rita pulled at Flora's jumper, afraid of what might happen next. Fearing that her little friend might suddenly receive a bloody nose or black eye as Fiona's face grew a deep shade of crimson.

Flora wrestled free from Rita's grip and stared blankly at Fiona, waiting patiently for her next move. The kids in the class were suddenly chanting Flora's name. She was the only kid they knew of that had ever had the nerve to face Fiona McPherson. As the tension grew, Miss Templeton entered the room.

Fiona turned on her heels and protested, "Flora is sitting in my seat!"

Miss Templeton peered above the rim of her glasses and replied, "the last time I looked Fiona McPherson, none of the seats had your name on it. Now sit down!"

Flora looked smug, but Rita knew that as soon as the bell went at break time Fiona would be waiting. Flora knew it too. In fact, she was counting on it.

The dungeon was everything that a dungeon ought to be. Dark, damp, cold and, as the children put it, "smelled like the contents of Father Ignatius' toilet."

Sister Ophelia pointed the light of her torch in every direction. The hole in the wall, where disobedient girls were placed, was thankfully unoccupied.

"Daphne!" called out the nun, her voice echoing in the vastness of the empty chamber.

A noise sent her spinning in the opposite direction as a beam of torchlight captured the backend of an enormous rat disappearing into an open pipe.

"Daphne, you down here?"

Sister Ophelia shivered dramatically, partly from the coolness of the air and partly from her fear of creepy crawlies, of which she suspected there were many.

She crossed the length of darkness, jumping at the sight of anything dangling and anything with more than two legs brushing the hem of her habit.

The search seemed futile. There were multiple places that Daphne could have concealed herself in the shadowy crevices of the stone walls, but one nun with one torch did not make a successful search party.

Sister Ophelia headed for the steps, climbed to the top, switched off the beam of light, and listened.

Within a couple of minutes, she heard the mumbling of a child's voice.

She descended silently one step at a time, hoping not to alert Daphne to her presence.

The voice grew louder as she crept forward into the darkness, stopping to listen after every step.

There, to the left of her, she sensed movement. The child's voice silenced. The nun spun on her heels and flashed torchlight across the area, hoping to find Daphne crouching in the intensity of its beam, but the space was empty, except for a lonely filing cabinet nestled beneath a maze of oversized webs.

Sister Ophelia shuddered. If the webs were that big, what size were the spiders that made them?

She daren't allow herself to think about it as she reached for the handle of the top drawer.

A web clutched at her hand, clinging aggressively as she tried to shake it loose. She brushed the remnants away with the butt of the torch and pulled the drawer towards her.

Inside was packed with decaying files. Water had sullied their descriptions and age had weathered their delicate exterior. Some disintegrated as she tugged at them, others clung beneath the paperclips that held them delicately together.

The nun flicked hastily through. The names were of children who had frequented the convent long before the current Mother Superior's reign. They dated back almost a hundred years to the very first child, Ethel O'Callaghan.

Sister Ophelia closed the drawer and pulled at the second one. There were merely remnants of files inside, paper jigsaws fashioned by age.

It was a miracle that anything had survived this place, thought the nun. And why were the files hidden beneath the convent, anyway? Shouldn't they have been destroyed years earlier?

The last drawer proved more problematic as it was locked.

That made Sister Ophelia even more inquisitive. What was so secret that it had to be locked away? She could only imagine that it was something she was not supposed to find.

She tugged at the third drawer, but time had not desecrated its lock. It sparkled with newness against a patina of rust. Someone had placed it there recently, hoping its secrets would never be revealed.

The nun hammered at the lock with the base of her torch, but it made no difference. The drawer remained secure.

She scoured the floor beneath it for signs of a key, but sadly did not discover one.

Then she happened upon a silver hair grip half buried in an inch of dust. She thrust it into the lock and jiggled. Breaking into a locked drawer was far harder than she had thought. The first couple of centimetres of the hair grip snapped off, but the nun was undeterred. She wrestled with her makeshift key until she heard a resounding click. Could that be it? Was the drawer unlocked?

She pulled at the handle as the drawer swung to freedom.

Inside lay a single file wrapped in a perspex sleeve, shielding it from decay. Sister Ophelia reached forward, pulling the file into view. The glow of torchlight highlighting the only word written across it 'FLORA'.

In the schoolyard at break time, Flora was pushing Rita on the swing. Fiona was approaching with determination in every stride.

She stood at the side of the frame and glared. Flora paid her no attention and continued pushing Rita higher and higher.

"It's my turn now," demanded Fiona.

"No, it's Flora's turn," replied Rita as she hopped off the swing, allowing Flora to take her place.

"I'll push her then," declared Fiona, shoving Rita aside, where she stumbled and fell backwards onto the wet grass. Fiona laughed as Rita climbed to her feet and inspected the green patch that decorated the back of her skirt.

"Looks like you've wet yourself," she smirked, her eyes disappearing momentarily behind huge bloated cheeks.

Flora felt the dark shadow rising inside her. She was unafraid as she flew higher and higher, and the momentum of the swing picked up speed.

Rita began to panic. The swing was likely to turn 360 degrees if Fiona continued. Flora would take flight over the top and almost certainly hit the ground from a great height, but Flora didn't seem concerned. Flora felt safe, knowing that her dark shadow was in control.

The swing went up and almost full circle. Flora clung on. It went again, this time making a full loop over the top of the frame. Flora didn't nose dive to the ground. She sat firm and waited. As the swing made its descent, she stuck out her feet and aimed them at the torso of the awestruck Fiona. Fiona lifted into the air and flew towards the railings at the edge of the playground. She hit the spikes with full force, impaling herself on the metal fence. The sound of her backbone snapping brought a smile to Flora's face.

Occupants of the playground froze as Rita's screams alerted staff to the tragedy.

Fiona's blood soaked the grass, dying the cluster of daisies growing there a deep shade of pink. Her eyes were open and staring. She choked on the severed contents of an artery as Flora watched the life drain out of her. Flora's smiling face was the last thing she saw. Fiona McPherson was dead!

XX

Sister Ophelia concealed the file she found in the dungeon beneath her habit. "I don't think Daphne's in the dungeon," she revealed, emerging from the bowels of the convent, "though without proper lighting it's impossible to be certain."

"Is there anything you can tell us, Agnes, that might help in finding Daphne?" questioned Sister Grace.

Agnes shook her head.

Daphne was usually a reliable child, level-headed and had shown natural leadership to the younger children. She was occasionally prone to bouts of depression and could be obsessive about certain things, which would ascribe the word 'tenacious' to her personality, but Daphne had never gone missing before.

"Should we inform the police?" proffered Sister Maread.

The nuns threw questioning glances in her direction. If Mother Superior were here, she would certainly not approve of involving the police, but then she wasn't and a decision had to be made.

Sister Ophelia nodded, confirming the suggestion to be appropriate.

A single telephone call brought two elderly officers to the convent's door. They asked a few questions and took a description of the child, then left muttering that if she hadn't returned by morning, a detective would likely make a visit.

"Well, a fat lot of use they were," declared Sister Maread as she closed the door behind them.

"I suppose there's a chance that she could turn up," added Sister Grace. "I think we should pray for her safe return."

As the sisters headed towards the chapel, Sister Ophelia detoured to her bedroom, where she hid the file inside her pillowcase.

Father Ignatius was stumbling along the corridor as the nun headed to prayers. Despite his incoordination, he seemed more lucid than usual. Alcohol did not emanate from his breath and his speech was not slurred. It was merely age that sullied him.

"Sister, I've been looking for you," he called.

"Really, Father, and why's that?" replied the nun.

"The other night when you asked about exorcism. I feel I was abrupt, aloof about the subject. You obviously had an interest to ask in the first place and I apologise for my attitude."

"That's quite all right Father," replied the nun softly, "I had heard that you were once in the exorcism business yourself and my curiosity was misplaced."

"No, Sister, it is important not to stop questioning. I should be happy to engage with you on the subject if you so wish?"

Sister Ophelia abandoned prayers and accompanied the old priest to his quarters.

It was the first time she had stepped inside his living quarters, as he spent much of his time in the Holy Mother's office befriending the bottles that lived in her glass cabinet.

"Sit down please," began the priest, poking the embers of a dying log fire back to life, "now what would you like to know?"

Sister Ophelia seized the opportunity. She knew that a sober Father Ignatius was a rare commodity and this moment may never present itself again for a long time, if ever.

"I'd like you to tell me about your life as an exorcist and why you chose the position?" she began.

"One doesn't choose to become an exorcist, Sister. IT chooses you!"

The nun smiled questioningly.

Father Ignatius settled in the chair closest to the fire and wrapped a blanket across his arthritic knees.

"I was a young priest, fresh faced, ready to go to war for God. I had a small congregation in a quaint fishing village on the north side of the island. One day, a member of the parish called for me to visit their child, a boy aged eleven. They said he was afflicted and they needed my prayers."

"I thought they meant the child was ill, and my presence was requested as a means of comfort. When I arrived at the house, it soon became clear to me that the child was possessed. I had no experience in such matters and I pleaded with the family to let me call in an exorcist from Rome, but they begged me to intervene, fearful that their son had only the night to live unless the evil was cast out. I was out of my depth. I'd only seen one video on the subject and I knew that one wrong move could kill us all."

"Oh my goodness, what did you do?" enquired the nun as she absorbed every morsel of the priest's story.

"I took out my Bible, a small bottle of holy water and my cross. I blessed each item and prayed to God for guidance. I crossed to the bed where the boy lay and blessed him signing the cross over his forehead. Almost immediately, deep welts scorched his skin as the sign of the cross burned into him. He writhed and thrashed beneath the prison of his bindings. He spat and hissed at me. Profanities soiled his speech, the like of such I had never heard before. His eyes glowed red and broken Latin flowed eloquently from his mouth. Not spoken by the child himself, but by the entity that possessed him."

"Were you not afraid, Father?"

"Afraid! I was quaking beneath my cassock," sniffed the priest, "my holy water was gone in one swift movement of my trembling fingers. Such was the fear that possessed me, but I persevered. I knew the consequences if I did not. I could not fail the innocence of the child on the bed. I placed my crucifix on his body and read aloud from the Bible, and I kept on reading until the child's body stilled. I'm not sure how long I was there, but by the end, there were no windows left in the room, no mirrors or light bulbs unbroken. The bed had collapsed, and the experience left each of us a little more aged than before, myself included. Until that night my hair was dark brown, but when I left the house I was completely white."

"You saved the child and cast out the demon?" pleaded the nun.

Father Ignatius shifted in his chair, his eyes filled with emotion as he answered, "I did indeed and he went onto join the clergy himself I believe. As for the demon, there is always another waiting to take its place."

"And that's how you became an exorcist?"

"Well, the Vatican was so impressed by my ability I became a member of the International Association of Exorcists. From then on I travelled to wherever I was needed."

"There were obviously others," began the nun. "Were they all as successful as your first one?"

"I'm afraid not, Sister. I lost as many as I saved and over the years, that became a very large number indeed," replied the priest solemnly.

Sister Ophelia had witnessed a fleeting glimpse of the man Father Ignatius had once been. Courageous, persistent, a lifesaver. She would never again frown upon his drunkenness or beg him to restrict his thirst. The priest had earned the rites to dampen his memory with liquor.

"You look tired Father, perhaps it's time for you to rest?"

The old priest smiled politely. "I never rest, child. The demons make sure of that."

Sister Ophelia wasn't quite sure what that meant, but she thought it best to leave the man alone. His eyes were heavy with sleep.

"Sister, is there a reason you asked about exorcism?" The priest's voice questioned wearily.

The nun hesitated for a moment, then smiled softly and shook her head, "good night Father."

XXI

Sister Ophelia raced back to her bedroom, eager to unveil the file she had concealed beneath her pillow case.

She heard the Mother Superior's voice in the corridor, reverberating the same old indignant tone. She was obviously home from her journey.

In the confines of her room, the nun tossed the contents of the file onto her bed. It wasn't as exciting as she had first hoped, though it contained more details than the previous one.

Flora's mother, Marley Sutton, was mentioned. Her address was listed as the vicarage in Ballykilne. She was only fifteen when she fell pregnant with Flora, nothing but a child herself.

Flora's father's name was not mentioned at all. Marley's parents' names were written on the back of an envelope containing a letter. Judging by the unbroken seal, the letter had never reached her and its contents gone unseen.

There was one other item, stuck in the corner of the file, a photograph of a young man. The nun assumed the image was that of Flora's father, though it bore no details or inscription. The man was handsome, dark-haired and slim. There was a hint of familiarity about him, especially the eyes, though he resembled no one the nun had ever met.

Sister Ophelia removed the loose floorboard beneath her bed and concealed the file inside. It seemed the only safe place no one was likely to look. She said her prayers and blew out the candle.

It was barely dawn as the sound of screaming echoed through the convent. Sister Ophelia leapt out of bed.

In the corridor opposite Mother Superior's office stood Sister Grace, her nightgown soaked with blood, and standing beside her was Daphne holding a rather large knife in her left hand.

"What has happened?" cried Sister Ophelia, approaching the duo.

Sister Grace could not speak, but pointed to the open door of the Reverend Mother's office.

Sister Ophelia stepped inside. It was difficult to visualise anything in the dimness of lamplight and she did not know what she was looking for. She moved around the desk, catching something hard with a stub of her toes. The sole of a black shoe stared up at her. The shoe belonged to a foot, and the foot to the Reverend Mother, who lay bathed in her own blood at the foot of the desk.

Sister Ophelia gasped with horror as the Holy Mother stared at her with lifeless eyes. There was no reason to feel for a pulse, but she did it anyway. Kneeling beside the blood-soaked body, she witnessed the multiple stab wounds decorating her torso. There were far too many to count.

The Holy Mother had been murdered. The Holy Mother was dead!

A congregation had gathered in the corridor now as news of the tragedy spread amongst the sisters.

"Has anyone called the police?" asked Sister Maread, as practical as ever.

Sister Grace was in shock. The answer was likely to be no.

Sister Ophelia turned her attention to Daphne, who stood bewildered, still clutching the knife.

"Daphne, where have you been?" muttered the nun softly.

Daphne pointed to the Reverend Mother's office.

"You've been in there the whole time?"

Daphne nodded.

"Were you hiding?"

Again Daphne nodded.

"Did you see what happened?"

Daphne glanced at the knife that was dripping with the aftermath of her actions.

"Did you do that to the Holy Mother?"

Daphne indicated she had.

There was no rational explanation for Daphne's actions. The police removed her from the convent for questioning. All that she repeated was, "she told me to do it."

Daphne never embellished on that sentence, and the truth of the matter remained unresolved. A court deemed Daphne insane and committed her to a children's mental facility.

A couple of weeks later, Sister Ophelia found herself sitting outside the hospital for the mentally insane. It was the place that now housed Daphne. The child's swift departure from the convent had left no time for explanation or interrogation. The nun had many unanswered questions. Uneasy thoughts that raced through her head and deprived her of sleep. Daphne's last words haunted her thoughts. What did they mean, and who was she referring to?

The room was pleasant and bright. Soft music hummed in the distance, and the children were immersed in activities.

Daphne was sitting at a table with a paintbrush in her hand.

"Hello Daphne, what are you painting?" asked the nun as she approached and took a seat beside her.

Daphne paused for a moment, then suddenly turned to Sister Ophelia and flicked the paintbrush towards her. A splatter of red decorated her habit and the side of her face. Daphne giggled mischievously. The nun was shocked.

Daphne lifted the brush a second time, but before she could repeat the task, a man in a white uniform grasped her hand.

"That's enough Daphne, paint nicely or not at all," he commanded.

Daphne was smirking as she pulled her hand free of restriction.

The man handed Sister Ophelia a paper towel.

"I'm sorry about that, Sister," he apologised.

"It's alright," replied the nun, removing the red liquid from her cheek.

"You're the first visitor Daphne has had. We never know what the reaction will be the first time around," explained the uniformed man.

"It's good to see her. She looks well," remarked Sister Ophelia. "How has she been?"

The man gestured towards Daphne's artistic display. The nun rose and moved towards him. From there, she could take full advantage of Daphne's artwork. The image was disturbing, depicting a little girl in the centre of the paper with yellow hair and black eyes. The rest of the paper was painted red.

Sister Ophelia threw a questioning glance towards the man.

"Rather gruesome, isn't it?" he remarked. "She paints the same picture every day!"

The nun returned to her seat beside the child. "Daphne, who is your picture of?"

Daphne, without breaking concentration, muttered beneath her breath.

"I didn't quite hear that. What did you say?"

The nun edged forward, leaning closer to the child.

Daphne's voice grew louder and louder until she was screaming maniacally, one word repeatedly, 'FLORA!'

The man in white lifted Daphne from her seat and carried her towards an exit. Sister Ophelia hurried on behind.

"What's wrong with her?" she cried.

"Nothing that a little shot won't take care of," replied the man.

In an instant Daphne was sedated. Laying on a bed with her eyes closed.

As the man in white left Daphne's beside, the nun was waiting.

"I've never seen her like this before. She lived at the convent for four years," explained the sister.

"Mental illness is a monster," began the man, "one minute she's a quiet, angelic child and the next she's... well, exactly what you just witnessed. The metamorphosis is instant. We don't know what triggers her?"

"Have you asked her about it?" enquired the sister.

"Asked her? Sister, the child hasn't spoken a word before today."

Daphne's behaviour perplexed the nun. Could it be the trauma of Flora's sudden departure from the convent that manifested this change in her? After all, the painting was an image of Flora and they had been very close.

"Would you say Daphne is right or left-handed?" asked the nun suddenly.

Without hesitation, the man in the white coat answered with a definite, "right."

"That's what I thought," added Sister Ophelia.

"Is there a reason you ask?" queried the man with a frown.

Sister Ophelia shook her head.

The night of Mother Superior's murder, Daphne was holding the bloody knife in her left hand.

It was an unusual trait. The right hand dominated most children, as the nun had suspected was the case for Daphne. There was only one child, the nun knew whose predilection lay on the left. That child was Flora.

Daphne's painting of the girl with black eyes surrounded by an ocean of red plagued the nun's thoughts. Could the painting and her last words being 'she made me do it' symbolise Flora's involvement? She shuddered to think it could be true, but she'd had her own unnerving encounter with Flora at the Moreton's house. The face that had stared down at her from the bedroom window was not one of angelic innocence.

Could Edward Trent's opinion of the child be accurate? Was a black soul hidden behind the angelic smile and baby blue eyes.

She shook the thought from her mind, scolding herself for allowing it to enter.

She needed more answers. She needed to meet Flora's mother.

XXIII

Fiona McPherson's untimely death was deemed a tragic accident. Rita was traumatised and didn't return to school for several weeks. The sight of Fiona's blood devouring a small portion of the playground and the expression she had witnessed on Flora's face haunted her thoughts.

Flora was questioned by the headteacher and gave a perfect account of how the accident had happened.

Sitting like a china doll on a blanket of brown leather in the head teacher's office, Flora, wide eyed and angelic, the epitome of innocence, described the events leading up to Fiona's death.

"... and I couldn't stop the swing. It was too fast, and she pushed me so high." Flora had produced just the right amount of tears to fall slowly down the side of each cheek, a heart wrenching symbol for the adults who hung on her every word.

"Fiona was standing right in front of me as the swing came down and I knocked into her," sobbed Flora, "and that's how she ended up on the railings."

"There, there now, Flora, don't upset yourself," soothed the headteacher, handing out tissues and a warm hug, "none of this is your fault. Fiona's tragic death was an accident and nothing more."

Flora was excused, as sympathetic voices cooed and fussed behind her.

She wasn't crying now. The act was over. The tears had dried and a sly expression of accomplishment superseded the angelic innocence.

She told herself that it was the work of the dark shadow that lived within her, though she had to admit that she had gleaned a certain amount of pleasure from Fiona's horrific death.

Flora was becoming more aware of the darkness and she was beginning to like it.

Sister Ophelia, taking full advantage of the fact the convent had not yet been designated a replacement

Holy Mother, set off across Ireland to Ballykilne in search of Flora's birth mother.

It was a small village sitting on the west coast with a population of less than five hundred.

A long coach journey followed by a short taxi ride to a quaint guest house on the outskirts of the village brought the nun to her destination.

"What brings you to Ballykilne, Sister?" asked the owner upon her arrival.

"It's just a temporary stay in seek of one of God's flock," replied the nun tactfully.

"Would you have a name for the one you seek?" queried the woman as she peered above the rim of her glasses. "I know everyone in Ballykilne and thereabouts."

Sister Ophelia avoided the question with one of her own. "Could you show me to the room? I'm exhausted from the journey and need to lie down for a while."

Within minutes, the nun was sitting on the bed of a pleasant, chintz inspired bedroom. There was a washstand in the corner and a toilet next door. The window held the image of a church spire, the church where Marley Sutton's father had been, and could still be vicar.

The following morning, and a hearty breakfast later, Sister Ophelia set off toward the church.

She wandered through the graveyard, a smattering of headstones standing on a neatly manicured lawn. Some had been weathered by age, a couple were shiny and new. The nun read the names Herbert Locke, Mary Kilkenny and Niamh Sutton aged thirteen.

Perhaps the child was related to the Sutton family? A sibling to Marley?

The door to the church was open, and an elderly woman was arranging flowers beside the pulpit.

"I'm looking for the Reverend Sutton," declared Sister Ophelia.

"You'll find him in the vestry," answered the woman without hesitation.

The vestry door lay agape as the nun pushed inside. The room was warm, a lively fire danced in the grate, and the smell of charred wood and furniture polish filled the air. A white-haired man was poised beside the window, lost in thought.

The nun cleared her throat. "Excuse me..."

The man turned instantly, a look of surprise flickered in his eyes as he realised the nun was standing there. "Sister! I'm so sorry I didn't hear you enter," he apologised.

The nun closed the vestry door and took a seat.

The vicar offered refreshments. Sister Ophelia politely declined.

"What brings you to Ballykilne, and more importantly, to my church?" he enquired.

The nun, in that moment, was quite uncertain how to begin. She'd made the journey but hadn't really thought about how she would approach the subject of Flora, Vicar Sutton's illegitimate granddaughter or Marley, his shameful daughter.

"I'm looking for someone," she began, "someone I think you know."

The vicar took a seat opposite her, his eyes wide with anticipation.

"I'm looking for your daughter, Marley," declared the sister.

The old man edged forward, his eyes glazed with tears. "You and me both, Sister," he declared.

The nun was taken aback. She hadn't expected the vicar's response.

"You mean you don't know where she is?"

The old man shook his head, "I'm afraid not, Sister. The last I saw of her was the day she drove away to that convent on the other side of the island, and I've regretted it ever since." The old vicar bowed his head with despair.

"St. Catharine's?" queried the nun.

The old man's eyes flickered with expectation. "You know it?"

"Yes," nodded the sister, "I've journeyed from there."

It was obvious the years had mellowed the white-haired man. Regret was his bedfellow now. Whatever his religious belief, Marley was still his daughter. He had sent her away in haste. Pride had rendered him blind to the feelings of his heart. He'd already lost one daughter, lying yards away in the graveyard. He longed to know of Marley's whereabouts. He longed for the chance to recompense and make amends.

"You have no record of where she went after the convent?" he pleaded wearily.

"I'm afraid not," replied the nun, shaking her head, "but I know of your granddaughter, Flora."

"Flora?" he spoke her name with tenderness. "Flora was my mother's name. Marley loved her so." He was smiling now as memories flooded his thoughts.

"Can I see her? I must see her! You know where she is?" he brimmed with renewed hope.

Sister Ophelia sighed heavily.

"There's a problem?" he demanded.

"Not a problem as such," came the reply. "Let me tell you what I know, Father. Perhaps then we can discuss a reunion."

The old man listened excitedly to Sister Ophelia's words. At first he was enthusiastic, like a child hearing a new story for the first time. Later, he became disillusioned. Frowning with disappointment and disbelief.

"I don't understand...?" he questioned. "Are you implying my granddaughter is evil?"

"Evil is a very strong adverb," replied the nun. "Flora is... different from other children. She possesses certain abilities I have never seen before in a child."

The old vicar rose from his seat and paced the room.

"God-given abilities, as in she performs miracles?" he questioned.

"Miracles, yes. God given? I can't say for certain," replied the nun.

"Where is she now?" queried the vicar.

"She's in foster care. She's safe and happy."

The vicar's face suddenly lit with excitement. "I'm her grandfather, and Thelma, my wife, is her grandmother. The child has a family of her own. She does not need to live with strangers."

Sister Ophelia knew at once where the conversation was leading. She did not think that Flora living with fragile, elderly grandparents was a good idea.

"What's wrong?" asked the vicar, "you appear opposed to the idea."

The nun had not revealed the most disturbing side of Flora's behaviour. Perhaps she had given the vicar false hope.

She countered his statement with, "what of Flora's father?"

The vicar grimaced. "I know only that Marley disgraced herself with him."

"You have no idea who he may be?"

"All Marley would say was that it was a man she met one night. A single encounter that demolished all our lives. She was rebelling, experimenting, brainwashed and manipulated by a group of good-for-nothings who had turned her away from God."

There was a hint of piety in the vicar's words. A glimpse of the younger man who had turned his pregnant daughter away. A sanctimonious preacher whose standing in the community meant more to him than his own kin.

Age and passing years had weathered the old vicar. He struggled with the decision he had made. He was repentant of his sin, not specifically for the treatment of his daughter, but for his own salvation.

Sister Ophelia stood and crossed the room. There was nothing more to say. The vicar knew nothing useful. It was time to leave.

"I shall fight for Flora, Sister!" his parting words followed her out of the church. Such a shame you didn't fight for your daughter, thought the nun to herself.

Back at the guest house, the nun took tea in the conservatory as she contemplated her meeting with Vicar Sutton. It seemed pointless to stay an extra day as she had planned. She had nothing further to report to Edward Trent, nor did she know where else to turn for information on Marley Sutton. She left the decision in God's hands. Should he have further need of her in Ballykilne, then she would stay, otherwise she would return to the convent the next morning.

Sister Ophelia closed her eyes for a moment of prayer, only to be disturbed by the clatter of china.

A young woman was clearing the table beside her.

"Sorry to disturb you, Sister," apologised the woman with a Scottish brogue.

The nun glanced towards her and smiled. "God has surely listened and has heard my prayer," quoted Sister Ophelia.

As their eyes met momentarily, the nun was struck by the distinctive colour of the woman's eyes. The piercing blue that stared back at her was instantly recognisable. She had only ever seen it once before in the child, Flora.

Sister Ophelia looked closer. The woman's hair was the colour of the night sky, except... shining beneath its darkness, a solitary curl had sought freedom. A golden lock announcing its existence for a fleeting moment before it was pushed hastily out of sight behind the woman's ear.

The dark hair was a wig, a disguise. Could this woman be Flora's mother standing right beside her?

"Marley?" uttered the nun. The woman didn't respond, but her body stiffened slightly as though the name had stirred an emotion within her.

Sister Ophelia touched the woman's arm. "Marley?"

This time, the woman turned to her. The nun knew the face immediately. It was Flora's ten years into the future. She knew at once that she was looking upon the face of the child's mother.

"Are you Marley Sutton?" asked the nun.

"Who?" replied the young woman.

"Come now, child, you know it's a sin to lie, especially to a nun," commanded Sister Ophelia.

The woman flushed with colour, but shook her head defiantly. "Ain't no Marley Sutton here. Never heard of her."

She was about to turn and walk away.

Sister Ophelia gripped her arm. "I know your daughter, Flora."

F ollowing the death of Fiona McPherson, Rita could no longer trust Flora. In their bedroom at night, she would turn away from her. At school, she would avoid her advances. Flora had noticed a difference in her friend. The Rita she had first met seemed to have abandoned her.

"Why don't you like me anymore?" she asked Rita one evening as they were getting ready for bed.

Rita shrugged, "I do like you, but..."

"But what?"

"I saw you hurt Fiona McPherson."

"I didn't do it on purpose," boasted Flora with a mouthful of toothpaste, "if she hadn't pushed me so hard on the swing, I wouldn't have knocked into her."

"I suppose not," replied Rita, shrugging.

Rita knew what had happened, and she'd seen the delight on Flora's face as Fiona's lifeless body straddled the iron railing. Rita feared for her own safety. She thought of the saying she had heard before, 'keep your friends close and your enemies even closer.'

That's exactly what she would do.

It was the first day of the summer holidays and the Moreton family were packing up to drive across the island for a holiday.

They were staying in a guest house on the edge of the coast with views across the rolling Irish sea.

"Isn't this wonderful?" cried Mrs M as she herded the children onto the beach.

They busied themselves making sandcastles, dipping their toes into freezing sea water and searching for crabs in rock pools.

Flora was enjoying the moment. Nothing bad was going to happen, she promised herself. She wouldn't allow her dark shadow to make an appearance.

Rita had thrown a kite into the air. It was bobbing and weaving in the breeze. Rory had just been attacked by an oversized crab and was waddling his way back to Mrs M, who was enjoying the sunshine in a striped deckchair.

A smaller girl had joined Flora in the rock pool with a green bucket and fishing net. She was a couple of years younger, pretty, with brown ponytails and green eyes.

"Shall we go exploring?" asked her newfound friend, "I'm bored with sea creatures."

Flora nodded excitedly.

The girl looked towards her parents, who were busily engaged in conversation with Mr and Mrs Moreton.

"Quick, before they see us," she giggled, grabbing Flora by the hand, pulling her along the beach toward the rocky cliffs in the distance.

They climbed for a while until eventually they reached the top, giggling as they did so. Both gasping for breath as they stood at the edge of the cliff and looked out to sea.

"I'm queen of the castle," shouted the child, spreading her arms wide.

"I bet you could fly!" suggested Flora.

"What do you mean?" questioned the young girl.

"If you jump off the cliff, you won't fall. You will fly like a bird," explained Flora, feeling the dark shadow rising within her. She tried to ignore it, but it wouldn't let her. It was growing stronger, controlling Flora like a puppet.

The girl looked skywards and pointed as a flock of seagulls raced overhead. "Like them?" she asked.

"Yes, just like them. If you hurry, you'll be able to catch up with them," encouraged Flora.

"Are you sure?" queried the girl. "It's an awful long way down if I fall."

"You won't fall, I promise, but if you do, I'll bring you back to life," replied Flora calmly.

"You can do that?" questioned the girl naively.

"Yes, I have special powers."

"Like a fairy godmother?" exclaimed the child.

"Exactly like a fairy godmother," vowed Flora.

The girl thought for a moment, "don't you want to come with me?" she asked.

"No, I've done it before. All fairy godmothers can fly silly!"

The girl hesitated, then stepped forward. Flora was close behind her, whispering encouragement in her ear.

A distant voice suddenly caught their attention. It was the girl's parents and Mrs M. on the beach below.

"Look, your parents have come to watch you fly," revealed Flora.

The girl waved enthusiastically and, without a second glance, hurled herself from the top of the cliff.

Of course, she didn't fly, but nose dived straight into the water below.

Flora watched as the child's frantic parents swam towards her.

From her vantage point, Flora observed the girl bobbing up and down in the water. She wasn't moving, her ponytails sinking, the green bucket floating beside her.

Flora smiled, knowing that the rescue was futile.

Suddenly the child was back on the beach with adults fussing around her and blue lights flashing in the distance as emergency services rushed to her aid.

It was too late. The child was dead. The impact from the height of the fall had rendered her unconscious, and she had drowned before her parents reached her.

Flora had climbed down from the top of the cliff now. Mrs M buzzing around her, spewing questions, "oh my goodness Flora, are you all right? Did you see what just happened to that little girl? What were you doing up there on your own?"

"I was trying to save her," sniffed a teary Flora. "She thought she could fly. I told her not to..."

"There, there, now deary. Don't get upset, it's not your fault," soothed Mrs M.

Flora sniffed and sobbed so dramatically that the nearby paramedic suggested she was in shock.

No-one questioned Flora's involvement any further. No-one except Rita.

In the quietness of the guesthouse bedroom, Rita turned to Flora.

"You told her to do it, didn't you?" she accused.

"What are you talking about?"

"The girl on the cliff, you told her to jump."

"I most certainly did not," growled Flora. "I was trying to save her."

Rita turned away, disgusted by the answer. She was certain she knew the truth.

"You better watch what you say, Rita," threatened Flora, "if you think I'm so bad you should be careful."

Rita kept her distance following the cliff incident. She didn't trust Flora at all. There was a tone in her voice that frightened Rita. A change that would take hold of her as though a powerful, invisible puppet master were at work.

Rita said nothing.

She watched silently as Flora grew more powerful, both at home and at school.

There was a monster lurking behind the innocent smiles, a darkness growing in the pretty blue eyes.

It was only a matter of time before Flora revealed her true self. Rita was sure of it.

Flora was two different people. Rita had heard talk of that about one of the other foster children. Bipolar was the word the adults had used. One minute happy, smiling and pleasant, the next minute moody, sombre and nasty. Perhaps Flora couldn't help the way she was. Perhaps Flora was ill. No one else seemed to realise. Only Rita had witnessed Flora's true personality.

Rita prayed silently each night that Flora would leave the Moretons so she could feel safe again.

XXIV

T he young woman paled at the sound of Flora's name.

"You know my daughter?" she muttered softly.

"So you are Marley Sutton?"

She shook her head. "Marley Sutton died eight years ago when her child was cruelly ripped from her breast. My name is Blair Duffy now."

The Scottish accent and the wig were a ruse to cover her real identity.

"She looks just like you," revealed the nun. "Same eyes, same hair."

"Is she still at St. Catharines?" whispered the woman.

Sister Ophelia shook her head. "No child, she is in foster care."

Marley Sutton's eyes widened. "I have so many questions, but not here, Sister. Meet me tonight at this address." The woman placed a paper napkin in the nun's hand.

The nun nodded. She had many questions of her own. Perhaps tonight they would both get the answers they were seeking.

As a veil of darkness enveloped Ballykilne, Sister Ophelia left the guesthouse. Lamplight scarcely lit the village and navigating the country lanes was challenging. She had exchanged her habit for more comfortable attire and appropriate footwear. She did not want to bring undue attention to herself as she roamed the village after dark.

She followed the bend of the lane, turning left at the village shop, then travelled a length of bushes to their conclusion, finally stepping onto a gravel driveway where a small cottage stood alone in the shadows.

She knocked at the door and waited. The latch lifted, and Marley Sutton's golden curls bounced into view.

"Come in, Sister, please take a seat," she ushered the nun inside before checking the vicinity around the cottage for unexpected visitors.

The home was compact and cosy. The warmth of a log fire danced in the hearth. Tartan plaid curtains and scatter cushions in autumnal colours decorated the room and an abundance of heavily framed pictures of the Scottish highlands adorned the walls.

"You have been working hard at convincing people of your roots," remarked Sister Ophelia.

Marley smiled. "It was the only way to throw them off the scent. If anyone had an inkling of who I really was, then my father would beat down the door."

"Then why come back here? I mean, you could have gone anywhere, as far from here as possible?"

Marley's smile faded. "I wanted to be close to my mammy," she admitted soberly. "This way I can see her, hear her voice, even talk to her without revealing my true identity."

"Even your mother doesn't suspect it's you?"

"I don't think so," hesitated Marley. "If she does, she's kept my secret."

"And your father?"

Marley sighed heavily before replying, "when I left for the convent, I had dyed my hair bright purple. Before that it was jet black, green, pink, every colour except my own. It was my defiant phase, as father called it. I'm not certain he remembers the real colour of my hair. I was rebelling against him and the church. A teenager with a chip on her shoulder and all the answers to everything. You know the kind. I disappointed him, brought shame upon the community. For those reasons, I avoid him at all costs. I don't think he would want to see me, anyway."

"God teaches us forgiveness child, after all, he is the ultimate source," consoled the nun.

"Perhaps, but I fear too much time has passed and there are too many sour memories for either of us to truly forgive," replied Marley.

When the small talk was over and they were both armed with coffee cups and chocolate biscuits, an air of awkwardness followed. Both had many questions. Bother eager to begin. Neither sure of who should speak first.

"Well," began Sister Ophelia, breaking the silence, "I have many questions for you, my most important being; who is Flora's father?"

Marley almost spilled coffee over the carpet. Her face drained of colour and her eyes glazed over. Perhaps she was not expecting such a direct question?

"I'm sorry," added the nun, "if it's too painful to talk about."

"No, it isn't that," replied Marley. "He's just someone I have tried so hard to forget. He's become a figment of my imagination. I convinced myself that he never existed, that Flora never existed. It's the only way I can survive."

"That's quite understandable, child, and I wouldn't have asked, but it's rather pertinent to answering questions about Flora."

"What kind of questions? Is Flora all right?"

This time it was the nun's turn to hesitate. "The truth is, I really don't know. On the one hand, she is all right, but on the other, she's not."

Marley grimaced with concern. "Was she born with defects, disabilities? I only saw her for a fleeting moment...!"

"No, nothing like that," interrupted the nun, "physically she's a perfect little girl, angelic, beautiful, but..."

"But what? Is she brain damaged? Was it the drugs, the alcohol, the cigarettes?" Marley threw her arms in the air and paced the room.

"No, she's not brain damaged Marley, she's..."

Marley stopped and turned on the spot, her eyes searching for answers in the face of the nun who sat before her.

Sister Ophelia fumbled for the words, finally choosing, "she's different," as her description.

"Different how?" pleaded Marley.

"Come sit down, you're wearing out the carpet," begged the nun.

Marley obeyed and took a seat. She was physically trembling, emotionally distraught.

Sister Ophelia searched for the words to best explain the young woman's daughter without sending her spiralling out of control.

"She has a special gift, you see…"

"Oh, thank God! Sorry, Sister," apologised Marley, basking in relief. "You mean she's talented? Intelligent? A protégé?"

The nun shook her head. "No, none of those."

"Then what?" cried Marley impatiently.

Sister Ophelia breathed deeply. She knew that what she was about to say would sound like madness. "She can bring people, birds, dogs… back to life!"

Marley dropped to the floor and grabbed the nun's hand, kissing it desperately. "God has forgiven me for my sins," she wailed, "he's blessed my daughter with the gift of miracles."

The nun waited for Marley to stop celebrating. "Is it not something to be thankful for, Sister?" she pleaded. "Why do you look so worried?"

"Flora has indeed been blessed, though I am not certain it was by the hand of God."

"What do you mean, is it not a miracle to give life to the dead? Is it not God that grants such miracles?" Marley suddenly stopped as the words left her mouth, "if not God... then... Satan?"

She raised her head towards the nun and dropped her hand as though a sudden revelation had grown inside her.

"Oh my, oh my, oh my!" she chanted repeatedly.

There was significance in her distress.

"What is it Marley?" pleaded Sister Ophelia. "Help me to help Flora, before it's too late."

XXV

Flora was playing in the garden on the day a white-haired old man approached. He stared at her from a distance, then waved her towards him.

Flora was hesitant. The man was a stranger. She shouldn't approach.

The man smiled warmly and waved again. Flora checked behind her that no one else was watching. She stepped cautiously forward until she reached the gate.

"Hello," said the man.

Flora studied him. He was old and wrinkled, his teeth stained yellow and his eyes bloodshot behind black-framed glasses.

"What's your name, child?" he questioned.

Flora stayed silent. She felt uneasy, just like when Mother Superior dragged her out of bed to scold her or place her in the dungeon.

The old man leaned forward. The knot of his coloured scarf falling loose to reveal a white collar around his neck.

Flora jumped backwards. She didn't know why, but she knew that the man made her feel uneasy. Her stomach cramped as though her dark shadow was wrestling in turmoil. She needed to get away from the old man as quickly as possible. She ran towards the house, screaming for Mrs M.

"Whatever's the matter, child?" cried Mrs M as she hurried out of the kitchen with cheeks the colour of fire.

"There's a man in the garden," pointed Flora excitedly, "a strange man."

Mrs Moreton rushed to the door. There was a man, as Flora had stated, a good man, a vicar.

"Please come inside," proffered Mrs M. "Can I get you some refreshments?"

"Thank you kindly, my dear lady, but I just came to see my granddaughter," replied the man.

Mrs M was taken aback. She'd had no previous call to say a relative was visiting, least of all one she had never met before. It was most irregular for someone to turn up unannounced. After all, there were processes to follow about such things.

"Forgive my ignorance, but how do you know that your granddaughter lives here?" queried Mrs M.

"I've just this minute spoken to her," he replied, "the pretty girl with the angelic face."

Mrs M was confused. Never in the time she had fostered Flora had she heard mention of grandparents.

Flora had disappeared from view, obviously unsettled by the old man's arrival.

"I'm sorry Mr...?"

"Father Sutton." he held his hand forward in a gentlemanly manner.

"I'm sorry, Father Sutton, but I cannot allow you to see your granddaughter until I have spoken to social services."

The old man appeared disgruntled. "How preposterous. I've travelled from the other side of the island to see her," he groaned.

"Well, I'm sorry about that, but you've had a wasted journey, I'm afraid. Rules is rules and I don't intend to break any on your behalf."

Father Sutton stepped forward. "What harm would it do for the child to spend five minutes with me?"

Mrs Moreton stood her ground. "I have no evidence that tells me you are her grandfather, sir!"

"Does this not speak for itself?" he touched the white collar around his throat. "I am a man of God. What better evidence could you need?"

Mrs M rolled her eyes. The conversation was getting tedious. "As I said, sir, I have no proof of who you are, man of the cloth or imposter you won't be seeing no child today. Now, may I bid you farewell?"

"No, you may not, woman," growled the old man, "I'm here to see my granddaughter and I'm not leaving until I do!"

"Adam!!" called Mrs M loudly.

Adam appeared in an instant at the sound of his mother's voice, "please escort this gentleman to the door."

Adam didn't need telling twice. He hooked his arm around the old man's and almost dragged him across the hallway.

"I must protest!" shouted the vicar.

"Protest all you want," replied Mrs M, "it's my son or the police. Take your pick."

It took a certain amount of effort for Adam to haul the old man off the property. He certainly wasn't the weakling he appeared. There was strength in his elderly muscles and buckets of determination as he wrestled to free himself from Adam Moreton's grip.

"You haven't heard the last of this," he threatened as he staggered towards the garden gate.

"Go through the correct channels and next time you will be more than welcome," stated Adam.

As the gate closed behind him, Mrs M came hurtling across the lawn. "How did you know our address?" she balled, but the old man kept walking and didn't respond.

"What was that about?" asked Mr M as he arrived home from work to find his wife and son barefoot in the garden.

"Someone demanding to see Flora," replied Adam.

"Without an appointment?" questioned Mr M as he watched the back of the old vicar disappearing down the street.

Mrs M was flustered and took a certain amount of calming.

"I'll ring the authorities later," declared her husband, "can't have people appearing out of nowhere claiming to be a grandparent. It's not fair to us and it's certainly not fair to the children."

Flora had been watching from the bedroom window. She'd heard most of the conversation between Mrs M and the old man. She couldn't imagine that she had a grandfather, and she was certain that if she did, it wasn't him.

"Why was there a vicar at the house?" asked Katrina, giggling as she entered the bedroom. "Was he here to save your soul, Rita?"

"Not my soul," replied Rita sharply as she tossed an accusing glance towards Flora.

Flora paid no mind to either girl. Her thoughts were still occupied by the white-haired old man. She couldn't forget the feeling she'd had when she saw his white collar. She felt as though she were being ripped in half, one half feeling good about him, the other feeling hate. The latter being the strongest.

Suddenly, she had an urge to reach for the Bible. A compulsion to prove something to herself, but it wasn't in its usual place on the bookshelf.

"It's on my nightstand," revealed Mrs M. "You can get it if you want to."

Flora didn't hesitate.

She found it sitting beside Mrs Moreton's silver-rimmed spectacles in the place where she had said.

Flora lifted it carefully and held it for a moment, staring at the title embossed across the black leather in gold letters.

The longer she held it, the warmer her hands felt until the heat was so hot it was burning her fingers and palms.

In an instant, the black leather turned fiery red as the book burst into flames. Flora dropped it to the ground and squealed. Her hands scorched by the intensity of heat that had engulfed them.

"What's wrong?" cried Mrs M as she entered the room in a hurry.

Flora held her hands forward, but the blisters had disappeared. Her hands were unscathed.

"That's no way to treat the Bible," groaned Mrs M, picking it up and replacing on her bedside table.

Flora looked on with disbelief. She had just seen the Bible burst into flames. It burnt her hands, but the black leather cover was unmarked and her hands were healed.

This had never happened to her before. She had been forced to read the Bible daily at the convent without incident.

Flora felt confused. She went to bed but couldn't sleep. Why didn't the Bible like her anymore?

Did it mean she was a bad person? Did it mean that God no longer loved her? Flora felt more alone than ever before as she struggled to find comfort in sleep.

XXVI

Marley Sutton poured herself a brandy. Her hands shook and her voice trembled as she began her story.

As a child, Marley had been trapped inside the vicarage with an overly religious, strict father and timid mother. She longed to break free and experience life her own way.

She hated the title of Vicar's Daughter and rebelled against the church, turning her back on religion. She dyed her hair black, painted her fingernails the same colour, applied over zealous amounts of makeup, and redefined her image.

The more her father hated it, the more she continued to rebel against him. Constantly disappointing him with her choices. She took up smoking, drinking and had a penchant for recreational drugs.

In the summer of her fifteenth year, she met Christian. A handsome guy with a highly addictive personality. He was a couple of years older, and had found religion in another form. Boasting it to be the one true religion.

Christian wanted to share this experience and introduce Marley to, as he called it, 'a life-changing experience'. Marley couldn't refuse him. It was almost impossible. His hypnotic eyes and beguiling smile held her under his spell.

A couple of weeks later, in the cellar of a large Manor House on a cold winter's evening, Marley was invited to meet Christian's cultic group.

She had no idea what to expect. Religion for her had always taken place in a church building, not the bowels of an old mansion. The drive from Ballykilne had been short, yet Marley did not recognise the surrounding area.

The house itself was imposing and eerie, sitting amidst extensive gardens and huge fountains. Large stained glass windows, whose depictions had faded with age, lit its façade. Overgrown vegetation clung delicately to centuries old crumbling stonework as the gothic architecture wrestled against nature.

Marley was uncertain. The house frightened her, and she hesitated as Christian's car pulled to a stop in the driveway.

"Do you live here?" she questioned.

"Sometimes," replied Christian without embellishment.

Marley climbed out of the car. A brisk wind caught hold of her and she shuddered at its sharpness. The moon shrank behind a passing cloud as if the sight of the house had scared it away. A magnitude of ancient trees swayed violently in the distance, moaning painfully.

Christian took hold of her hand. "You're shaking!"

Marley felt the voice of her conscience whispering words of caution as she reluctantly followed Christian towards the house.

They didn't enter by the front, bypassing the huge arched doors heading down the side of the building instead.

Here there was shelter from the wind, but the path was winding and slippy with fallen leaves. Only darkness led the way.

At the back of the house and in the openness of its far-reaching gardens, Christian unlatched a heavy metal door and forced it aside.

Marley glanced into the dark passageway ahead and back towards Christian, her eyes questioning whether it was safe to enter.

"Sorry," groaned Christian, "I'll turn the lights on."

In one respect Marley wished he hadn't, perhaps she would have felt better entering the passage in darkness. Cobwebs hung from its vaulted ceiling, dampness dripped down its moss-covered walls, and the smell was indescribable.

"Are you sure this is it?" demanded Marley as Christian nudged her forward.

"Of course I am silly, been here hundreds of times," came the reply.

The passageway wound downwards, part slope, part steps. Marley picked her way carefully. A startled rat crossed her path, and she almost crumpled to the floor as her ankle gave way and she slid forward.

"Careful," whispered Christian, catching hold of her arm.

The sheer black blouse she wore did little to keep her warm. She wanted to impress Christian, but wished she'd abandoned the idea for a thick woollen jumper and scarf instead.

"How much further?" she queried, skating through puddles of green slime.

"Nearly there. I promise you it'll be worth it," boasted Christian.

Suddenly the air changed as a warmth enveloped her. Candlelight flickered in the distance as they headed towards their destination.

The room was small, well lit and filled with people. Ordinary people, who were swaying and chanting, holding hands in a circle as they moved in harmony with each other.

Christian's face was beaming now, his eyes glowing excitedly in the candlelight.

Marley glanced towards the floor. It was patterned with weird shapes and symbols.

The chanting stopped. Silence filled the room. Christian tapped Marley on the shoulder and pointed forward.

In the centre of the circle, a man rose to his feet. Marley had been unaware of his presence until then. He was tall and lean, his naked body covered only by a cloak. He was probably middle-aged, though Marley couldn't be certain. In his hand he held a bronze cup, which he raised into the air. He spoke a language Marley didn't recognise, then took a sip from the vessel.

He passed the chalice to the nearest person, who also drank of its contents and passed it on.

It journeyed around the room, finishing with Marley.

Christian offered her the cup, but Marley shook her head.

Everyone had turned to stare at her, their eyes hypnotic, their expressions inanimate.

Christian tried again, almost forcing the cup into her hand.

"Please," begged Christian, pouting dramatically, "it's only wine."

Marley hesitated momentarily, then placed the chalice to her lips. The taste was warm and sweet, much thicker in consistency than wine. It embraced her like a mother's hug and she felt herself smiling as she pulled the cup from her lips.

Christian nodded approvingly and that was the last thing she remembered.

She awoke on an unfamiliar sofa the next morning, in a room dripping with gold leaf and antiques.

A grand piano occupied space beside French windows and an enormous fireplace devoured one wall of the room decorated by carvings of hideous creatures.

"Whose house was it and how had she got here?"

Judging by the amount of daylight that shone into the room, she had spent the night here. Her father would be furious.

A door in the farthest corner of the room opened and a tall, handsome man entered, followed closely by her new friend, Christian.

"Good morning," began the man, "how are you feeling?"

Marley hadn't really thought about it, but now that she did, she actually felt pretty good.

"I imagine you have questions?" continued the man. "Christian, fetch your friend a cup of tea. I'm sure she's feeling thirsty."

She was parched actually, but hadn't realised it until that moment. She was hungry too, craving toast with lashings of marmalade.

"Bring toast and marmalade too," added the man.

He was intriguing. Could he read her thoughts? It was almost as if he were part of her, breathing the same air, understanding her requirements.

Christian reappeared with a tray of refreshments.

"This is my house," began the man, "a family inheritance, an heirloom, passed down to me by my grandfather. One day it will be Christian's," he patted the young man on the shoulder and smiled.

"It's very lovely," acknowledged Marley, lifting the fine china carefully, gulping at its contents and refilling the cup as though she had just spent a week in the Sahara without liquid refreshment.

"Sorry I'm so thirsty," apologised Marley.

"My wine does have that effect, I'm afraid," suggested the man, who had now taken a seat beside her.

"Are you Christian's father?" enquired Marley, observing the same chiselled bone structure and undeniable attraction.

The man smiled and nodded. "I am his father, but not biologically speaking. I am his Redeemer, his God, his Truth and his Salvation."

Marley felt confused, but didn't feel comfortable enough to question further. She smiled politely and tucked into breakfast.

"Last night was the first step to your own deliverance," began the man.

What was he talking about? Pondered Marley.

"I'm talking about the second coming, Marley," declared the man.

Marley's mind was spinning uncontrollably.

He was inside her head, invading her thoughts, exploring the crazy whirlwind of inexplicable questions that queued for answers.

"I shall give you the answers. Don't worry," he replied.

Marley laid the toast aside. It was delicious, but the man was beginning to unnerve her. How did he do that? Was she imagining this whole scenario? Where these people real or had she succumbed to an accidental overdose of drugs and entered a world beyond? Was she dead?

"No, of course you're not dead!" stated the man sternly. "You have much to live for, my dear. You shall bear the saviour of the world."

Marley was heading for the door now. She needed to leave, clear her head, breathe some fresh air, and collect her thoughts. She was panicking, bewildered, claustrophobic in this atmosphere. Her pulse was racing uncontrollably. She felt faint, nauseous, reaching for the door handle, but it didn't turn, it was locked. The keyhole sat empty. Marley was trapped.

XXVIII

F lora's grandfather was not about to abandon his only grandchild. He left the Moreton's house with increased vigour and renewed determination.

He could go through the proper channels. He could wait for the justice system to analyse the situation. That would take months, something that he didn't have. Vicar Sutton had recently been diagnosed with pancreatic cancer. His earthly journey was almost over, but he certainly wasn't going to end it without saving his granddaughter.

When Thelma Sutton, his ill-fated wife and devotee for the last half a century, found out about Flora, she was delighted. Having already lost two daughters, the thought of a granddaughter renewed her passion for life.

They hatched a plan and the following week, the Vicar and his wife set off to County Bottega.

Thelma waited anxiously outside the school gates.

"You won't be able to miss her," informed her husband. "She's the image of Marley."

The statement was accurate. As the sunlit curls of a beautiful blue-eyed girl bounced into view, Thelma had no doubt that she was gazing upon her granddaughter for the very first time.

She had to work quickly, though. The fire alarm was still resounding as children spewed into the schoolyard from all directions.

Thelma seized the opportunity in the turmoil of wide-eyed children and panicked school staff as they tried desperately to restore order.

She grasped Flora's hand gently. Flora turned towards her and tried to shake free, not recognising the woman beside her.

"It's alright my darling. Don't be afraid, I'm your grandmother. I'm here to save you," whispered Thelma.

"Save me from what?" asked Flora, confused.

"From the fire that's about to engulf your school and burn it to the ground."

Flora focused on the ribbons of smoke curling upwards from the first-floor windows. A sudden explosion blew out the glass, scattering shards across the playground.

"Quickly, we must leave now, before you get hurt," enthused Thelma, tugging gently at the child's hand.

Flora obeyed. There was something benign about the woman, almost familiar. They hurried from the chaos without detection and jumped into the waiting vehicle of the old vicar.

Flora landed on the backseat with a thud, as the car skidded away at speed.

"I know you," shouted Flora, pointing at the vicar with an accusing finger.

The vicar nodded, "yes I'm your grandfather, your mother's father!"

"I have no mother," protested Flora moodily.

"Of course you do," insisted the vicar.

"No, I don't. I was born in a convent. Is that where you're taking me?" queried Flora anxiously.

"No, child, we're taking you home, to our home. A place where you will be safe, where we can look after you."

Flora didn't trust the man with the white collar. He made her feel funny inside. He upset her dark shadow, and she knew that when the time was right, she could deal with him. The old man didn't frighten her in the least.

Flora was silent for the rest of the journey. She wasn't sure where she was going, though she knew it wasn't to the convent or the Moreton's house.

Flora awoke as the car ground to a halt. She rubbed her eyes and yawned. From the window she spied a pretty house, much smaller than the convent but built out of the same material. It had a green door and roses growing in the small expanse of garden that framed it.

It didn't look too bad, perhaps even a little exciting. A feeling she wasn't used to experiencing. She jumped from the car and followed the old couple inside.

It smelled of boiled cabbage and lavender. Its decor was pleasant and welcoming. Big armchairs filled with fluffy cushions, flower patterned wallpaper and curtains, green plants and a fireplace that was bigger than Flora herself.

Flora headed for the stairs, closely followed by Thelma. She dashed from one room to the next, throwing open wooden doors, exploring inside and giggling as she did so.

The last room was her favourite. A white wooden bed furnished with teddies, pink curtains and rainbow wall paper. A soft patterned rug and shelves full of different sized dolls.

There was a dressing table too, mirror and rocking chair by the window.

"Do you like it?" asked Thelma, who had been hovering in the doorway, absorbing her granddaughter's enthusiasm.

"It's so pretty," replied Flora, throwing herself onto the bed, wrapping herself in the softness of the blankets.

"This was your aunt's room," declared her grandmother fondly.

"I have an aunt?"

"You did, but sadly, she is no longer with us."

"Why, where is she?" questioned Flora innocently.

Thelma crossed the room to the window. She pointed outside towards the church and the small graveyard.

"She's dead?" proffered Flora as she gazed upon the tombstones.

"I shall take you to meet her tomorrow," enthused Thelma.

"I can bring her back to life if you want?" declared Flora without hesitation.

Thelma smiled sweetly as she stared into the azure blue of her granddaughter's eyes.

"That would be lovely if you could, dear, but she resides with God now," sighed Thelma.

"I can though, I've done it before..."

"That's nice, dear," dismissed Thelma as she hurried Flora from the room. "Now let's make you some supper. You must be starving."

Flora hadn't thought about it until now, but yes, her stomach was rumbling like the ancient water pipes in the convent.

That night Flora lay in a warm, cosy bed with a pretty nightlight for company and the two dolls she had chosen to sleep with her.

The lady who called herself grandmother had been especially kind. She'd made gingerbread men for supper with hot chocolate and marshmallows. It was as if she had been waiting all her life for a granddaughter.

Flora turned towards the window, pulling the warmth of the quilt around her, gazing upon the moon as it smiled down from the night sky. Perhaps Flora would like it here, perhaps she would even fit in. She hoped so. She hoped that she didn't do anything bad. She didn't always want to, but she didn't have total control. Sometimes the dark shadow that lived inside her was too powerful to ignore. Flora closed her eyes and drifted into sleep.

XXVIIII

"Why is the door locked?" demanded Marley nervously.

"Locked! Is it really? It isn't usually," replied the tall man.

He crossed the room towards her. Marley stepped aside anxiously as he reached for the handle.

The door swung open immediately.

"You mustn't have turned it fully," smiled the man.

Marley felt paranoid. She could have sworn that the door was locked.

Noting the glimmer of doubt in her expression, he added, "besides there isn't a key, so it couldn't be locked."

Marley smiled tentatively and nodded her head.

"There's no need to be nervous, Marley. I'm not going to hurt you or hold you prisoner. I merely want to help you."

Marley strayed from the door back towards the fireplace. "Help me, why? How?"

"Trust me, child, you're going to need it. In a couple of months, everyone will know your secret. You'll be an outcast in your own community, but you will be welcomed into mine."

Marley felt confused and more than a little hazy about the night before.

What was the man talking about?

"I'm sorry I don't understand," she began. "What is happening in a couple of months?"

The man smiled wilfully, "you are with child my dear. You shall be mother to the Saviour of the world."

Marley's head was spinning. She felt nauseous. What on earth was he talking about? Hadn't that already happened? It was recorded in the Bible. Mary was mother to the Saviour of the world.

"You are correct," declared the man reading her thoughts again, "this child, however, shall takeover the world. This child will possess the ultimate power to destroy the weak and strengthen the bold."

Marley slipped onto the sofa, lost in thought.

How could she be with child? She had tried many vices, granted, but sex hadn't been one of them. She drew the line where that was concerned. She wanted her first time to be with the love of her life, not a drug induced low life with pimples on a stained mattress by the railway bridge.

Marley wasn't perfect by any stretch of the imagination, but she did still live by a certain moral code.

"You look unwell," stated Christian, who until that moment had said nothing.

There was a sudden moment of insight as Marley's brain jumped into overdrive.

The wine the night before, it's consistency and taste. It hadn't been wine at all.

She flew towards Christian and slapped him hard across the face. "You drugged me!"

The slap had been harder than she realised. Her palm stung, and Christian's face bore a bright red handprint across the right cheek.

Christian stepped forward and raised his hand to reciprocate.

"Let's not fall out, children," interrupted the man, grasping Christian's hand before it reached Marley's face.

Marley was raging with temper now. Fall out! She was ready to kill Christian with her bare hands. He had ruined her, not just physically, but her future, her name and... her father. What would he think about this? He'd disown her. The shame would be too much for him. Until that very moment, she hadn't really cared what her father thought. He knew about the drugs, the alcohol and the smoking. She did it to upset him and it did, but she also knew just how far to push him. A pregnancy would all but destroy him.

"I'm going to the police," announced Marley. "Tell them you raped me."

"And I will tell them you consented," replied the man sarcastically.

Marley stopped in her tracks, her thoughts racing, her heart beating uncontrollably.

"Was it you? Did you do it?" she demanded.

The man didn't respond.

"Well, did you have sex with a fifteen-year-old? I'm underage, you'll be charged with paedophilia!"

The man smirked, "oh child, so feisty, yet so naïve, you have so much to learn about me."

Marley felt trapped, abused, dirty. She wanted to wash away the stench of the previous night. She didn't know what to do next.

She paused for a while, pondering her situation. She was a teenager, still a child in the eyes of the law. The year was 1969, she would be the talk of the village. Ostracised by the very people she had grown up with. Looked upon with shame. Labelled harlot, whore. She'd be sent away to a home for unmarried mothers.

"Yes, child, all of those things," declared the man. He'd been inside her head again, reading her thoughts.

"You and I are now connected spiritually. You carry a child that will be very special. A child that will change the world. A child I have been waiting for."

Marley eyed the man suspiciously. Was he now admitting to being the father, or was Christian to hold that title? Either way, one of them was responsible, or were they both? Had she been violated by both of them? The thought made her heave.

"I need to go home," she begged, holding a hand across her mouth. "I don't feel well."

"No one is stopping you," replied the man as he crossed to the door. "You won't go to the police!"

His eyes darkened as he stared into hers. For a moment, she thought someone or something else was staring back at her. The depth of his gaze filled her with trepidation. Something told her that going to the police would be extremely bad, but Marley wasn't one to back down easily.

"And what if I do?" she growled.

It happened within seconds, so quickly, in fact, that Marley hadn't even realised. She heard a scream and turned to see Christian engulfed by flames. She started towards him as he wrestled and squirmed with agony.

"Oh my God," she gasped, but there was nothing she could do. Christian hovered above the ground as fire feasted upon his body.

"Stop!" she cried out as Christian's remains showered the carpet with ash. There was nothing left of him, just a mound of dust where he had stood.

Marley was in tears now. She could not believe her eyes. She closed them and prayed that this was all just a dream, but when she opened them, Christian's remains still covered the ground.

"I thought he was your son!" she hissed.

"I have many sons, as many as there have been years," he smirked. "All are disposable, except for the child you are carrying. That one is special!"

"You're a monster," screamed Marley.

"I am indeed, and that is what will happen if you tell anyone," scolded the man, pointing towards the mound of ash, "to your parents, your friends, the police, whoever you betray me to."

Marley sank to the ground. Suddenly she yearned for her father, to hear his melodic voice advising her, his Biblical quotes to soothe her. Why had she wanted to hurt him so?

The man caught hold of her hand and pulled her upwards towards him. "You will never speak of me. You will never speak of Christian. You will bear this child and you will bring it to me. If you don't, I shall find you, I shall find the child and I shall destroy the world as you know it. The future is yours to determine."

There was a passion in his tone, a change in the pitch of his voice. His eyes were smouldering, a fiery red glow passed across them and for a fleeting moment Marley saw a face in them. Not the man's face, something so hideous, that she heaved up the contents of her stomach.

"I think I've made my point," stated the man ruthlessly.

"Who are you?" mumbled Marley.

"I," said the man, "am your worst nightmare!"

XXIX

Flora explored her new garden. Went on a shopping trip to the village and found an injured black cat just yards from the back door.

"Can I keep it?" she asked her grandmother, dispensing a bloodied bundle of fur on the kitchen table.

"I think it's beyond keeping dear," replied Thelma. "Looks like a fox has had a go at it, poor thing. I'm afraid the kindest thing would be to put it out of its misery."

Flora had no idea what that meant, but she left the cat with her grandmother, assuming she was going to make it better.

The next morning Flora found the cat dead in a black plastic bag beside the bins.

She felt upset that her grandmother hadn't helped the animal, but Flora knew exactly what to do.

"Come along dear, I'm going to take you to meet your aunt," Flora skipped alongside her grandmother as they headed toward the graveyard. At the headstone of her youngest daughter, Thelma laid a bunch of flowers that she had picked fresh from the garden.

"What happened to her?" queried Flora.

"She got ill, very ill. The doctors didn't know what it was. They couldn't save her," sniffed Thelma with tear-filled eyes.

"How old was she?"

"She was thirteen. Just had her birthday a couple of days before..."

Flora could see that her new grandmother was upset. "Do you miss her?"

"Oh Flora, I miss her so much. She was so beautiful. In fact, she looked just like you."

Thelma stooped and placed a tender kiss on Flora's forehead. "Now let's see about getting dinner made."

It was much later that evening when darkness had painted the sky a dusky grey that Flora left her bedroom and tiptoed through the house.

She unlatched the back door and stepped outside barefoot, dressed only in pyjamas.

The black cat she had saved from the bin bag was waiting for her. It purred and meowed around her legs, then followed her through the shadows to the graveyard.

Flora paused at the headstone of her deceased aunt, removed the posy of flowers and sank down onto the ground.

"Dig," she commanded of the cat, who dug its claws into the soil harrowing at the earth beneath, but the cat's paws made little impact on the grassed area. Flora tugged at the ground, unearthing meagre clumps of dirt and lawn.

"I don't think this is going to work," sighed Flora, who was beginning to tire.

She spread herself across the ground and whispered into the earth below.

"I don't think that will work either," she declared to the cat who had curled up beside her.

Flora yawned. Bringing people back to life was tiring.

It was the sound of a woman's anxious cries that broke her sleep. Thelma was standing over her.

"I've found her, she's here!," shouted her grandmother, breathless and dishevelled. "How long have you been out here, child? You'll catch your death," fussed Thelma.

Flora climbed to her feet, leaving the black cat exposed on the ground.

Thelma let out a scream.

"What is it, dear?" asked the vicar, who had joined them.

Thelma was speechless, but pointed at the black cat as it unfurled itself from sleep and stretched.

"That cat was dead. I placed in a bin bag myself."

"You must be mistaken. It couldn't have been dead, or perhaps this is a different cat?" reasoned the vicar.

Thelma grabbed Flora's hand and hurried her back to the house. She rummaged amongst the bin bags, but the cat wasn't there.

"See, it's gone," proffered a distraught Thelma.

"The fox will have had it. Now come on inside. Let me make you a nice cup of tea," comforted the vicar.

Flora hovered beside her flustered grandmother.

"It was me!" she declared with a smile. "I brought the cat back to life!"

"Don't be so silly that isn't possible," dismissed the vicar.

"Yes it is, I've done it before," continued Flora smugly.

"Lies is a sin child," warned the vicar, wagging his finger in her direction.

"It isn't lies," protested Flora, "I can bring things back to life."

"Go to your room immediately," ordered the vicar, "Ill have no such lies being told in my house."

Flora sat on her bed for longer than she cared to remember. Her stomach groaned with hunger and she desperately needed a bath.

"Stupid grandfather," she muttered to the doll who shared the left side of her pillow.

"Of course I brought it back to life. Why doesn't he believe me? Perhaps I need to find another way to show them."

The bedroom door opened, and the black cat padded across the carpet. It hopped onto the pillow and purred.

"You believe me, don't you?"

The cat ignored her and began preening itself.

The following day, with the events of the previous one behind them, Flora was helping her grandmother clean the house. Thelma was taking down curtains in the main bedroom to wash and clean the windows. It was a beautiful morning, warm for the time of year. The sun was shining. It was the perfect day for a spring clean.

Flora was removing ornaments from the windowsill as Thelma splashed soapy water across the glass.

"I think a bird has pooped on that window," pointed Flora at the spatter of black and white paste that smeared the outside glass.

"So it has," replied Thelma, opening the window, "not to worry dear, I think I can reach it."

Thelma balancing on a small footstool hung out of the window and reached for the unsightly stain.

"Hold the stool, dear," called Thelma as her wet cloth hit the glass.

Flora bent to steady the stool as it wobbled violently beneath the weight of her grandmother. Thelma scrubbed at the glass, complaining about the stubbornness of the stain.

She hadn't noticed the black cat until it hopped onto the windowsill, when she caught sight of it through the glass. Thelma screamed, the stool wobbled uncontrollably and, losing her balance, she dropped from the window onto the patio below.

Flora's head poked through the window. "Grandmother!" she called, but the old lady did not respond.

Flora swung round and headed for the stairs.

Thelma was not breathing. Her eyes were wide and staring and a stain of blood haloed the top of her head.

Flora shook her, but there was no response. Thelma was staring at the sky, eyes fixed. Thelma was dead.

Flora knew that look. There was only one thing to do.

She knelt beside her grandmother and breathed upon her. Then muttered something into her ear and waited.

It seemed like an age before Thelma moved. She was cold to the touch. The sun had moved direction, disappearing to the other side of the house, leaving them in the coolness of the shadows. Flora hadn't left her grandmother's side, nor had the black cat.

"Oh my goodness, what has happened?" cried the vicar, spying his wife on the ground as he arrived home for dinner.

"She fell out of the window," pointed Flora, looking upwards.

"Thelma, can you hear me?" exclaimed the old vicar, shaking his wife gently.

Thelma began to stir. At first she appeared dazed, disoriented. She rubbed at her head, covering her hand in congealed blood.

"Let's get you inside. I'll call Doctor Chamberlain."

Thelma insisted she was fine, and there was no need to trouble the good doctor.

"It's just a concussion," she insisted.

"How long had you been lying there?" queried the vicar as he dressed her wound with a bandage.

"Not long," came the reply as Thelma stared at him, unblinking.

The vicar was unaware that his wife had died three hours earlier. He put the kettle on, as that seemed to be the one thing that solved adult problems.

Flora watched her grandmother with interest, noticing how the black cat that she had been so terribly afraid of was now sitting comfortably on her lap. Thelma stroked it happily and smiled as it purred beneath her touch.

The vicar had noticed it too and it slightly unnerved him.

For the next couple of days Thelma appeared relatively normal, though she neglected her chores and spent most of the time nursing the black cat.

Flora basked in the glory of having secretly saved her grandmother and had even told her so. Thelma nodded her head, accepting everything Flora told her without hesitation or question.

"That's nice, dear," she uttered inanimately as Flora finished talking.

When the vicar arrived home for supper, none had been prepared.

When he challenged Thelma, she responded, "that's nice dear."

Flora felt no emotion towards the vicar, other than he made her feel uncomfortable, especially when he flashed his white collar. The dark shadow inside her grew with intensity each time he approached. Its distaste for the holy man was palpable.

Flora enjoyed watching the old man squirm as he tried desperately to navigate his way through the kitchen.

Supper that evening was dry crackers and cheese, and of course, a pot of tea.

On the fourth day after her fall, Thelma failed to leave her bedroom. She spoke of a headache and a bloody cough. The vicar was terribly worried, but Thelma soothed his concerns and insisted that sleep was all she needed.

The black cat slept beside her on the bed. In fact, anywhere Thelma was, the cat was too.

On the sixth day, Thelma emerged from her bedroom and appeared in the kitchen. The vicar was attempting to prepare breakfast. He paused as she entered and threw six rashers of bacon into sizzling oil.

"How are you feeling dear," he asked without turning his attention from the bacon.

Thelma didn't reply, but moved closer until she was almost touching him. The vicar turned towards her, gasped loudly and stumbled backwards, tossing the contents of the frying pan into the air.

Thelma's appearance startled him. Glassy eyes stared from beneath furrows of hanging skin. Her face pale and gaunt, highlighting the skeletal structure of bone beneath. An emaciated body shrouded beneath a floor length nightgown that defined her frailty as she moved.

As the vicar moved further away, she followed. The sleeve of her nightdress brushing against the blue flame of ignited gas. Her sleeve and arm caught fire, but she didn't seem to notice.

Thelma continued towards him, fire engulfing a curtain as she passed. The vicar was stumbling backwards in fear of his own wife.

Suddenly the black cat leapt towards the old woman, landing on her right shoulder. Thelma turned to glance at it, displaying an open wound on the back of her head that wriggled to life with bloated maggots feasting on the necrotising flesh.

Thelma pushed forward as the vicar backed himself into a corner. He glanced towards Flora, who sat at the kitchen table, unperturbed.

"I told you I could bring people back to life," declared Flora.

The vicar pushed Thelma to the ground, covering her with a tablecloth, sending the fine china that sat upon it crashing to the floor.

He beat at the flames, but no matter how hard he tried, he could not extinguish the fire.

Grabbing Flora by the hand, he pulled her out of the house as Thelma wrestled beneath the fiery inferno.

They hurried towards the church, the vicar panting for breath as he pulled Flora beside him.

"Quickly inside," he ordered. "I will call for help from the phone in the vestry."

Flora hesitated as the dark shadow told her not to enter the church. The feeling was so strong it wrestled inside her. The dark shadow feared the sight of the church and all that it symbolised.

"I said quickly," snapped the vicar, pushing Flora inside.

Flora stopped dead as she crossed the threshold, planting her feet stubbornly on the worn stone beneath them.

Her eyes were drawn to the image of Christ impaled upon the cross.

She felt nauseous. Her stomach churning as she watched her grandfather disappear from view.

The darkness inside her grew stronger, its power surging through her body, engulfing every inch of her. The air grew cold, icy cold. Flora could see her breath. She was not alone.

A ghostly shadow crossed in front of her, the outline of a barefooted girl, whose trail of muddy footprints traced her journey towards Christ.

Flora knew her instantly.

The vicar emerged from the vestry, stopping in his tracks, his eyes widening, his mouth falling open.

The shadow stopped moving. It held his gaze as though he were hypnotised by its presence.

Flora moved forward.

The shadow turned. Flora's own face stared back at her, a little older perhaps, but with a definite resemblance.

"Niamh?" whispered Flora beneath her breath.

The ghostly figure didn't reply.

The vicar found his voice now. "It cannot be!" he quivered. "It's not possible," dropping to his knees.

Flora felt her mouth moving, but the voice that spoke was not her own.

"Anything is possible when you follow Baloid," it bellowed, reverberating throughout the church.

The shadow stretched a hand towards her. Flora accepted. Together they approached the vicar, who was crawling towards the altar clutching his chest.

He began to recite the Lord's Prayer, gasping for breath as he did so.

The shadow raised a hand towards him, lifting the vicar off his feet, raising him into the air, until he was dangling above the altar like a puppet.

The vicar's face grew pale, his eyes bulging, his voice faltering as he struggled to finish his prayer.

With a twist of its hand, the shadow spun the vicar upside down.

Then, without prompting, Flora and the shadow set the vicar alight.

How it had happened Flora wasn't sure, but she'd felt a great power emanate from her body.

They watched the vicar burn for a moment, then released his body to fall upon the altar. The cloth that covered it instantly set alight and within minutes, the whole church was ablaze.

"This is the judgement of hell," growled the shadow as she turned and disappeared.

M arley left the mansion and never spoke a word of what had happened or what she had witnessed to anyone. She was too afraid of the consequences.

She'd memorised the journey that night, but when she tried to search for the house again, she couldn't find it.

A couple of weeks later, she took a pregnancy test that yielded a positive result. She had to steal it from the pharmacy and hope she didn't get caught. Until then, she had passed the event off as a dream, a hallucinogenic result of drugs perpetrated by Christian or the man he called Lord. Living in denial was the simplest and easiest way for Marley to exist, at least until the positive test, which then changed everything.

As evidence of her pregnancy grew, she covered it as best she could. Her skirts wouldn't zip up, so she held them together with safety pins. The same happened with her jeans, which she disguised with baggy jumpers.

Then, as she neared her third trimester, there was no hope of concealing the extent of swelling beneath her clothes.

The night she told her parents was purgatory. So many questions. So many answers she didn't have and couldn't give. In the end, she told them that the father was an older man who she had met briefly and thought to be in love with. Of course, the man had a wife and a family, and she had been childish and naïve.

Her fate was now sealed. She was going to St Catharine's Convent for unmarried mothers where she would give birth to the child, which would be brought up by the nuns until adoptive parents were found.

Marley would return home when all signs of her shameful misdemeanour had vanished.

"And so, Sister, I could not return to the village and walk the streets with a label on my forehead. I feigned a new personality and here I am, Blair Duffy from bonnie Scotland."

The nun had to admit that the accent was impressive and believable, but the wig covering needed a little more care. Had it not been for that discrepancy, Sister Ophelia would have been leaving Ballykilne without answers.

"I'm so sorry," declared the nun soberly.

"I feel it was penance for my wayward behaviour," replied Marley.

"God would not allow you to encounter such depravity as a source of penance, my child," comforted the nun. "God forgives all sin and asks only for your love and devotion in return."

Marley nodded as she wiped a solitary tear from her cheek.

"You were meant to find this man and deliver your child to him?" proffered the sister.

"Yes. If I didn't, he said he would find me," repeated Marley.

"I think he may have already found Flora," declared the nun with a frown. "Not physically, but spiritually."

"What should I do, Sister?" pleaded Marley. "I cannot let him get his hands on her. I fear the consequences would be catastrophic."

Sister Ophelia agreed. Keeping Flora's whereabouts secret must be their priority.

"Do you think you would recognise the man who killed Christian if you saw him again?" asked the nun.

Marley was certain that she would. His face had been emblazoned on her memory since the events of their meeting. No matter how hard she tried to forget him, his image would not leave her.

"You believe the man to be Flora's father?" enquired the sister.

Marley nodded, "yes. I mean, no, I'm not certain. Why do you ask?"

"Flora's birth certificate bears Christian T as her father."

Marley had no idea. Christian was dead, she knew that, but it was the other man who demanded the child after birth. He was the one she feared.

Suddenly, headlights were flashing along the narrow lane outside Marley's cottage. Another passed, then another.

"Something serious is going on," declared Marley, grabbing her wig.

Together, they dashed out into the cool night air and followed the flashing lights and whirring sirens through the village. They stopped at the church.

"Oh my God," cried Marley, pointing at the church and then let out a scream as she witnessed her parents' home, both burning uncontrollably against the night sky.

"What's happening?" questioned the nun of a bystander in the crowd.

"The vicar's place and the church," he replied, "gone up in smoke."

"Anyone hurt?" begged Marley. The tone of her voice trembling slightly as she held her breath and waited for the answer.

"Sounds like Thelma's dead inside the house and the vicar in the church, though neither have been officially confirmed. I heard the fireman telling the police officer."

Marley bowed her head. She had always imagined a future reunion with her mother, once the vicar had taken his heavenly seat. There was no chance of that now. She was overwhelmed with emotion, which caught the eye of a couple of villagers standing close by.

Marley turned for a last look at the bonfire she had once called home. She glanced towards the church, its stained glass windows spitting fragments of colour into the darkness as they buckled against the pressure of the raging fire within. She thought of her sister lying beneath the ground. They will all be

FLORA

together now, she thought to herself. Niamh won't be alone anymore.

Marley couldn't pull herself away, looking over her shoulder as Sister Ophelia ushered her through the crowd.

In the corner of her eye and through the swell of tears, she was certain a small figure had crossed between the tombstones. She dismissed the thought as grief engulfed her.

Sheltering beneath the nun's embrace, she allowed herself to be guided home.

Flora watched from Niamh's graveside. Unaware that her biological mother and the nun who had cared for her were standing only yards away.

Flora turned, and without looking back, disappeared into the darkness.

XXXI

M r and Mrs Moreton were beside themselves with worry. They had alerted the appropriate authorities and the police when Flora disappeared and were anxiously waiting for news.

That arrived in the form of a phone call from the local constabulary. A local parishioner had noticed a girl in the graveyard with Mrs Sutton. She had given her quite the fright, as the child was the image of the Sutton's dead daughter, Niamh.

Flora's description had been circulated around the village, as had news of the untimely deaths of the vicar and Mrs Sutton. Flora had disappeared following the tragedies that befell her grandparents.

"So you've found her?" queried Mrs M nervously.

"Afraid that's a negative," replied the police officer, "the child has disappeared, but there is evidence that she had been living with the grandparents."

"You're certain she wasn't caught in the fire?"

"No madam, only two adult bodies were retrieved. No further human remains have been located," advised the policeman. "I dare say she ran away."

"Well, of course, she would be petrified," declared Mrs M. "Please keep looking for her."

The tragedy that had befallen Flora's grandparents was something of an enigma to the attending authorities, eventually labelled 'accidental tragedies.'

Rita had been listening to the conversation from the top of the stairs. She had a good idea of what had happened, and she was certain it would involve Flora.

It was a couple of days later that a police car pulled up outside the house. Rita watched from the bedroom window as Flora hopped off the back seat and was escorted into the waiting arms of a tearful Mrs M.

"Thank you, officer," she cried.

"Glad she's home safe," replied the policeman, "she's been through quite an ordeal lately, kidnap, death of her grandparents, found wandering on the top road. Probably hasn't eaten for days. Poor kid is bound to be traumatised. Needs a lot of love and TLC."

"Well, she'll get plenty of that here," announced Mrs M gratefully.

The family fussed over Flora, relieved and excited to have her home. That is, everyone except Rita.

One of the older foster children, Barry, had moved to a permanent residence. This freed up a bedroom, which the Moretons designated to Flora.

"She needs a bit of time alone," explained Mrs M when protests began over her choice of new occupant.

Rita was pleased. She would sleep easier knowing that Flora was across the hall and not in the next bed.

"We seem to have acquired a cat," giggled Mrs M as a black cat strolled into the kitchen and curled up beside the warmth of the oven.

"You survived!" shouted Flora excitedly as she spied her feline friend.

"You know the creature?" prompted Mrs M.

Flora nodded, "he lived at my grandparents. I thought he had died in the fire, but he found me!"

"Then we all have a new cat," declared Mrs M.

Everyone but Rita seemed excited by the fact. Rita knew that any cat of Flora's would be trouble and it took an instant dislike to her. Every time she approached, it hissed and clawed out.

"I don't think it likes you, Rita," observed Rory.

"I don't like it either," replied Rita. "It's mangey and full of fleas."

"Now, now Rita, don't be like that. He's our new pet," remarked Mr M.

Rita trusted the cat just about as much as she trusted Flora. She was going to keep well away from both of them.

"What's the matter with you, Rita?" asked Mrs M, taking the girl aside.

"Nothing," answered Rita.

"Is something bothering you? You used to be so happy and friendly. You and Flora were inseparable. Now you hardly even acknowledge her."

Rita played with her hands and rubbed the sole of her shoe up and down the carpet.

"You know you can talk to me, don't you?" reminded Mrs M. "I'm here for all of you children."

Rita thought for a moment before opening her mouth. "Flora scares me!" she blurted.

"What? Sweet little Flora? However could that angel scare you?"

"I've seen things she's done," announced Rita.

"I'm sure you've all done things I wouldn't approve of Rita, none of us are perfect, you know."

"Don't let her fool you, Mrs M," exclaimed Rita. "She may have the face of an angel, but she has the soul of a demon."

Mrs M was left in shock by Rita's revelation. She could only think that Rita's dislike of Flora was peer envy and nothing more. It was common amongst girls of their age.

She shook Rita's words from her thoughts and waved the children off to school.

XXXIII

Sister Ophelia headed back to the convent. News of a replacement Mother Superior had cut her trip short.

She'd left Marley Sutton to mourn her parents.

"Take as much time as you need," were her parting words to the young woman, "but when you're ready, come and find me."

Marley was keen to meet her daughter. She'd waited nearly eight years for that moment, a moment she never dreamed possible.

Though conceived by deceit, Flora was her own flesh and blood. She was excited by the prospect of becoming her mammy, but she couldn't shake the man's words from that fateful night. They still haunted her thoughts.

That horrible morning in the mansion, when he threatened her loved ones and vowed to find her if she didn't bring the child to him.

Marley told herself that the man may have left Ireland long ago, even died, though doubt haunted her theories.

She worried that if she were to meet Flora, would the man know? He appeared able to read her thoughts and feelings, but that was years ago, and she suspected that their connection was due to the unborn child growing inside her.

The funeral of her parents took place as Marley watched from the shadows, disguised as Blair Duffy. The finality was devastating. She could never make peace with them now, but she had the chance to begin a new chapter of life with her daughter.

"Welcome home, Sister. I have missed you so," declared Sister Grace.

"You talk as if I've been away for years," replied the nun with a smile.

"So it feels that way for sure."

"Now what news is there of the Holy Mother?" questioned Sister Ophelia, taking hold of her friend's arm.

"What is that saying? Better the devil you know," giggled Sister Grace.

"You mean she's going to be worse than the last one?"

The sisters laughed more loudly than was allowed in the hallowed halls of the nunnery, but as the new Mother Superior had not yet arrived, it didn't matter.

At supper, Father Ignatius was elated to see Sister Ophelia seated in the dining room.

"I knew there was something missing at the convent, Sister, and it was you," he declared soberly.

"That's very kind of you to say, Father. I trust nothing unusual has taken place in my absence?"

The priest shook his head, "thankfully no, I'm far too old for the unusual and probably far too tired to even notice, or is that too drunk," chuckled the old father, "perhaps you could check in on me after evening prayers."

The request seemed ominous, but the nun agreed.

Later that evening, Sister Ophelia entered the old priest's quarters. Lamplight flickered in the study where he usually sat as it was closest to his drinks cabinet. A fire glowed heartily in the grate, but Father Ignatius wasn't there.

"Father!" called the nun.

She hesitated to investigate the other rooms, one being a bedroom and the other a bathroom. It wasn't befitting for a nun to visit such places, even if the priest was 89 years of age.

"Father!" she tapped at the bedroom door. A light glowed beneath it. Perhaps the old man had fallen asleep and forgotten about their rendezvous.

A shadow moved across the light, paused for a moment, then moved aside. The sound of faint whispering caught her attention. She pressed an ear to the door and listened, but the words were not clear enough to make out. Was the Priest talking to himself? Perhaps he was praying?

"Father, are you all right?" she called.

Suddenly, the door swung open and Father Ignatius stepped into view.

"Forgive me, Sister. I lost track of the time," he mumbled.

The old priest shuffled towards his chair, stopped to prod at the fire, then took his seat, pulling a woollen blanket across his painful knees.

His face was flushed and his eyes glazed, much like they were when he had been on an alcoholic binge, but at such times the odour of alcohol was pungent, unmistakable, whereas there was no hint of his favourite tipple.

The old priest didn't speak a word. Almost unaware of the nun's presence.

"Are you feeling all right, Father? Would you be needing a doctor?" asked the nun.

"No, Sister, that won't be necessary. God is the only doctor I need. I'm ready when he sees fit to call me."

"Come now, Father, I'm sure he has more for you to do before then."

Father Ignatius stared into the fire and, for a moment, appeared to have drifted into sleep.

"I need to unburden myself, Sister," he muttered, "I need to do it now while I'm sober and still alive!"

Sister Ophelia stifled a wry smile. The Father had always been blunt and possessed a dry sense of wit, even now in his aging years. It was true the Priest was a shadow of his former self. Long gone was the dark-haired young man of twenty, ready to face the enemy, ready to fight for God.

"Whatever it is, Father, wouldn't you prefer a confessional?"

"No, Sister, you are the only one I can trust with these words. You are the only person who will accept and understand what I tell you."

Sister Ophelia pulled a chair closer. She felt a flutter of trepidation take flight in her stomach. Whatever was the old man was about to divulge?

Father Ignatius took a deep breath and began.

"In 1906, when I was no more than twenty years old, I was sent to visit a woman who had just given birth. My purpose there was to bless the child, but when I arrived at the house, I was told the child had died. I offered my condolences and offered the prayer for the faithful departed.

"I was told that it wasn't possible, as the child had already been taken away for burial.

"I was shocked. The family were devout catholics, but the mother was so distraught that I didn't like to question and prayed for their loss instead.

"As I left the house, I spotted an old woman hurrying down the lane with a bundle in her arms.

"I should have gone directly back to the church, but something impelled me to follow her.

"She traced a pathway over the fields and eventually disappeared through a stone opening shrouded by vegetation on the side of the hill.

"I hurried behind her, following down a damp tunnel that seemed to stretch to the other side of the island.

"As the tunnel forked, I saw light glowing from the mouth of a wide opening. I peeped inside just as the old woman was laying the baby on a stone altar. The child cried out as its tiny body made contact with the cold, hard surface. The old woman lifted a cup into the air and released a drop of coloured liquid into the baby's mouth. The child stopped crying, suckling at the nourishment it had received.

"A small group of people were huddled around the altar. They cheered, chanting a name as the old woman passed the chalice to each of them in turn."

The old priest heaved for breath and coughed momentarily.

"Here Father, water."

He sipped at the glass.

"Do you want to go on, Father, or are you too tired?" queried the nun.

"Tired or not, Sister, I must unburden myself. I must finish my story before death pats me on the shoulder.

"I never told anyone what I had seen. Perhaps I should have, but I feared no one would believe me. A young priest with a vivid imagination. It was only when I was introduced to exorcism and the many demons that roam this planet of ours that I realised I had witnessed a satanic ritual. Still, I said nothing, but I kept an eye on the child and watched him grow. To the outside world, he appeared as an ordinary boy, but I could see and feel the evil that grew within him."

The priest took another sip of water.

"Now, Sister, whenever that boy was near to me, I felt an alarm bell ringing in the pit of my stomach. The air grew colder and the light darkened. The boy became a man, and I lost all trace of him, that is, until just recently.

"As I strolled down the high street yesterday morning, I stopped to rest for a while. A man joined me. A man now in his sixties. The moment he took a seat, I felt it again, that alarm bell, the cold air, the darkness that accompanied him.

"He chatted politely for a while. Then he stood and touched my shoulder. I felt as though a stake had pierced my heart. Intense pain coursed through my body. I was paralysed beneath his grip, my lungs denied of air. He stooped and whispered, 'remember me?'

"As he released his grip, I was able to breathe again. I knew it was him, here in our town. Evil is living amongst us, Sister, and it must be destroyed at all costs."

"But who is this man?" demanded Sister Ophelia. "Do you know his name?"

The priest began coughing until a stain of blood appeared at the edge of his mouth.

"I do not know the name he uses to conceal his true identity, I only know him as Baloid."

A sudden chill coasted the nun's body. The name was familiar to her, but she could not remember why or where she had first encountered it. The old priest's tale was reminiscent of Marley's own encounter with evil. Perhaps the man they both spoke of were one and the same?

"Father, what does the name mean? Is it Irish?" begged the nun.

Father Ignatius dipped his finger into the blood oozing from the side of his mouth. He knew his time was short. On the back of his arm, he wrote the letters D I A B L O.

Sister Ophelia recognised it at once as one of the many names used to describe the devil!

Father Ignatius needed rest now and if breaking protocol was the only way to get him into bed, then the nun was prepared to face the consequences.

She covered the old father and said goodnight.

"Promise me, Sister, you will find this man and destroy him." His grip was hard, defiant.

"How do I do that, Father, guide me?"

"In my bureau, there is a file in a red binder. You will find everything you need to know in there. You must succeed, Sister. The fate of the world depends on it, but be careful he will not be easy to find and he will be even harder to destroy. You must have faith Sister, pray, believe, succeed."

The following morning at breakfast, it was announced by Sister Maread, that Father Ignatius had passed away in his sleep. The nuns fell to their knees and prayed for his soul.

Sister Ophelia had not found sleep an easy bedfellow that night, turning over Father Ignatius' words in her head. News of his death did not come as a surprise to her. The priest had foreseen his demise, hence the urgency to unburden himself.

She hurried to his study in search of the red binder, before his quarters were flooded with bereaved nuns.

Concealed beneath her habit, she carried the file to her bedroom and secreted its existence beneath the floorboards. It was not a suitable time to read it. Today was devoted to saying goodbye to Father Ignatius.

XXXIII

A social worker was visiting the Moretons that day. A social worker who brought exciting news.

"Flora's mammy has been located," declared the woman nonchalantly.

"Oh, I see," replied Mrs M with an element of surprise.

"You're not happy about that?" demanded the social worker.

"It's not that I'm not happy. Of course I'm happy for Flora, it's just that I didn't realise her mother had made contact."

"Following the death of the grandparents, her mammy, Marley, wrote to us. It seems she has been living in Ireland this whole time and had no idea what had happened to Flora."

"I see," sniffed Mrs M with emotion, "how soon will she be leaving us?"

"Well, there are procedures to follow..." began the social worker.

"Aren't there always," tutted Mrs M, much to the social worker's disapproval.

"Now I'll set up a meeting with Marley first, then a meeting with the two of you and Flora. If all goes well, then there will be several meetings with just Flora and her mammy, some assisted and some alone. At that stage and assuming mammy and daughter want to be reunited permanently, I shall issue a court order. Once that has the stamp of approval from a judge, then Flora will go to live with her mammy permanently. Is that clear?"

Mrs M cast a lip quivering glance to her husband. "It is," he answered on his wife's behalf, "we will miss her, though. She's an absolute angel."

"Aren't they all?" replied the social worker with a sarcastic tone. "I haven't been stupid enough to have any of my own."

"Then you don't know what you're missing," declared Mrs M disapprovingly.

The social worker packed her bag and headed for the door.

"Oh, don't mention this to Flora just yet until I've met with her mammy. I'm sure it will be fine, but don't want to make false promises now, do we?"

"Snotty bitch," growled Mrs M as she closed the door.

"Now mother, she's only doing her job," soothed Mr M.

"Well, she ought to take that lemon out of her mouth, sour-faced madam."

"Just because you disapprove of her manner doesn't mean she hasn't got Flora's best interest at heart."

"I suppose so," replied Mrs M. "I'm really going to miss that child, though."

"I know mother, me too."

XXXIV

It was the day of Father Ignatius' committal. The convent had been dressed in flowers in keeping with colours of the Irish flag. It was a tradition in the town when a patriot died.

It was also the day Marley Sutton arrived at the Beachcombers B&B.

With her parents gone, and a large insurance cheque expected, Marley wanted to put down roots in the area where her daughter was growing up.

"Are you from these parts?" questioned Mrs Brightman, owner of the establishment.

"Not originally, no," replied Marley tentatively.

Mrs Brightman was the best hostess in town, and she was also the nosiest. In exchange for a warm bed and a hearty breakfast, she expected to know everything about her paying guests from their shoe size to their favourite hymn.

"You'll be more than comfortable here," she boasted. "Breakfast is at 8 sharp. No guests in your room. Doors are locked at 10. There's a small bar downstairs and I can make you a sandwich before the kitchen closes at 6."

There seemed to be a lot of rules, but Marley nodded politely and handed over payment.

"Oh, if you want to use the pay phone, you'll need change and it doesn't accept the new 50 pence piece," informed the landlady.

Finally, Marley was alone to settle into her new surroundings. The Beachcomber sat in the very centre of the town whilst managing to back directly onto the beach. This had been achieved via an extension which was now the bar area Mrs Brightman had mentioned.

The room itself was warm, the bed covers thick and fluffy. There was a small clock radio atop a chest of drawers, a single wardrobe beside a sink, and a comfy chair positioned beside the window. The carpet was slightly worn in places, nothing that a rug wouldn't cover, and her window had a direct view of St. Catharines Convent.

It would certainly suit Marley's requirements whilst she looked for a property to buy. She'd had her furniture placed in storage for the time being and the one thing she had salvaged from the church, a large gold-coloured cross displaying the words:

FAITH IS THE STRENGTH BY WHICH A SHATTERED WORLD SHALL EMERGE INTO THE LIGHT.

It was her mother's favourite quote and, for that reason alone, deserved to take centre stage in Marley's new home.

The following morning, Marley sheepishly entered the dining room. To her relief, she was the only guest until about ten minutes later when a young man around the same age as herself took a seat at the table opposite.

"Morning Braden," hummed Mrs Brightman as she served up a full Irish breakfast.

"Thanks Mrs B," smiled the young man, who couldn't wait to sample the contents of his plate.

"Would you be wanting the same, miss?" asked the landlady, approaching Marley's table.

"Yes please," smiled Marley, "that would be lovely."

"Two ticks and you shall have it."

Marley tried desperately to avoid eye contact with the man. He was happily digesting his breakfast as if it was to be his last meal.

"Condemned, are you?" asked Marley jokingly.

"Sorry?" replied the young man, obviously not understanding the pun.

"I said, are you condemned? You're eating like it's your last meal."

"Oh, I always eat like this. I love food, can't help it. Sorry if it offends?"

"No, not at all," comforted Marley. "It's nice to see someone enjoying food so much."

"You can't help but enjoy Ms Brightman's cooking, it's amazing," added Braden, "just like me mam used to make."

The words 'used to' implied that Braden's mother was no longer alive.

"I've just lost mine too, both actually," revealed Marley.

"Lost both what?"

The conversation was becoming impossible. Marley scolded herself for making small talk with a stranger. The young man and she were obviously not compatible.

"It doesn't matter," sighed Marley.

The young man stood up, having finished his breakfast, and took a seat at her table.

"I'm yanking your chain," he grinned, "sorry, and sorry about your parents, too."

Marley blushed slightly. The warmth of her cheeks told her so. She felt like a schoolgirl again, but this time a respectable one.

"You here for business or pleasure?" asked Braden.

"Neither really," explained Marley. "I'm here to meet my daughter."

It was at that very moment that Mrs Brightman emerged from the kitchen with Marley's Irish breakfast.

"Married are you?" she asked in a waspish tone.

Marley shook her head.

"What's your daughter's name?" she asked boldly.

Obviously she had been listening at the door for sometime.

"Flora," replied Marley.

"Pretty name," added Braden. "I expect she looks like you!"

The compliment sent Marley into a spin. Her cheeks engulfed by fire.

Mrs Brightman laid down the breakfast plate, gave each of them a doubting glance, then disappeared.

"She means well, just has unbelievable hearing. I think at night she turns into a bat," chuckled Braden.

"Why are you here?" asked Marley as she tasted breakfast. It was every bit as good as Braden had described.

"I'm here to look around the university," he informed.

"Oh really, how exciting," exclaimed Marley with enthusiasm.

"I'm glad you think so,"

Marley would have loved to attend university. It was a part of her life she had missed, having had Flora so young.

"Why this university specifically?" asked Marley.

"I want to do a master's in parapsychology. The professor here is the best there is, apparently."

"That sounds awfully posh," joked Marley. "You must be very clever."

"Posh... no. I'm the son of a farrier. Clever, not so much, just interested in the unexplained."

Suddenly Braden wasn't so incompatible. He was easy to talk to, liked a joke and was pretty nice to look at.

As breakfast finished, Braden rose from the table.

"What are you up to later?" he asked with a wink.

Marley felt flattered. She was meeting the social worker at eleven, then calling at the convent to see Sister Ophelia, but she'd be free around five.

"Great, I'll meet you at the Coughing Donkey public house. You can't miss it in the centre of town. It's called that, but it boasts a picture of a goat, not a donkey at all."

Braden chuckled as he disappeared.

Mrs Brightman came to collect the empty plates.

"Watch yourself, deary, a young woman with a daughter out of wedlock. People talk around these parts. Young men and women fraternising, unmarried. You know what I mean? Don't want you ending up with a second illegitimate child."

Marley choked on her words. How easy it was for one person to judge another without availing themselves of all the facts.

XXXV

Sister Ophelia excused herself from breakfast on the pretence that she was feeling unwell.

"Nothing serious, I hope?" fussed Sister Grace.

"No, Sister, women's trouble if you must know!" replied the nun.

Sister Grace nodded knowingly.

In the confines of her bedroom, Sister Ophelia removed the red binder from its hiding place. She stared at it for a moment, her stomach churning. She grasped the cross of her rosary and looked inside. Father Ignatius' words had played continually in her thoughts since that night. The old priest had tasked her with an immeasurable responsibility. If, as he said, the devil walked amongst us, perhaps more importantly, walked in this town, then time was of the essence.

The binder surprisingly held very little information. A short verse from Luke 10:19:

"Look, I have given you authority over all the power of the enemy, and you can walk among snakes and scorpions and crush them. Nothing will injure you."

A page of scribbled notes and a photograph of a book, *The Philosophy of Demons*.

The last item was a letter from Father Ignatius which read:

Dear Sister Ophelia,

Read my instructions carefully. Memorise them and destroy this letter. Find the book. In chapter 13, you will find all the tools you need to exorcise the demon. Pray for your soul, Sister, and the souls of the innocents around you. Put on the full armour of God to stand against the devil's schemes.

God be with you, my child.

Sister Ophelia closed the file. How was she to find this book? Where was she to start? Father Ignatius had omitted to mention this in his haste to unburden himself.

She needed to visit Donal at the university library.

The nun was ready to leave the convent when Marley Sutton appeared on the doorstep.

"Marley!" she cried. "I presume it's Marley since you abandoned the wig?"

"It is," replied Marley, smiling.

"How nice to see you, especially in this part of our lovely country?" celebrated the nun. "I take it you're here to stay and meet your daughter?"

Marley nodded. "I've just been to meet a social worker. The wheels are in motion."

"That's wonderful news," replied the nun, embracing Marley with a sisterly hug.

"I'm on my way to the library. Walk with me," offered the nun. "How did your meeting go?"

Marley didn't answer straightaway, and when she did, she hesitated. "I'm not really sure, Sister."

"And why's that? Is there a problem?"

"Not a problem regarding me rekindling our relationship, but the social worker told me something that disturbed me."

Sister Ophelia stopped walking. "What is it, child?"

"My parents had kidnapped Flora from school. She had been living with them for a while. She was still living with them when their house and the church burned to the ground. When they were both killed. Flora walked away unharmed and is back living with her foster family."

Sister Ophelia was shocked. It was the second revelation she had heard in the last twenty-four hours.

"That certainly is disturbing," announced the nun. "You think Flora had something to do with it?"

Marley nodded, "I do, Sister. It's too much of a coincidence not to, especially after everything you disclosed about her."

Marley appeared deflated, her bubble of hope and reunion suddenly bursting with doubt and deliberation.

"Perhaps you should wait until you can meet Flora in person, ask her about it. All may not be as hopeless as you fear, Marley. There maybe a perfectly reasonable explanation."

Sister Ophelia didn't believe that for one moment, but for the time being, she seemed to have given Marley Sutton renewed hope.

"Thank you, Sister."

XXXVI

Rita hadn't seen much of Flora at all. She had acquired a new bunch of friends at school. Ones that smoked behind the bicycle shed and graffitied on the classroom windows.

Rita was happy that Flora had found new interests. It was the black cat that worried Rita the most.

It had a habit of sleeping on her bed. When she tried to shoo it away, it planted its claws firmly into the bedsheets and tore at them. She had even found cat poo on her pillow. The black cat didn't like her at all. It smelled like a dustbin, drooled green liquid from its mouth, and was losing patches of fur. It was more befitting of a horror movie than a family home, totally at ease in the role of zombified feline.

When Rita arrived home from school, the cat was on her bed as usual. She threw down her satchel and ignored it. It didn't move or hiss as she approached. Its claws were retracted. Rita moved closer. The cat wasn't breathing. She fled from the room to find Mrs M.

"The cat is dead!" she cried.

Mrs M didn't seem shocked. "Yes dear, the poor wee thing died this morning."

Rita felt confused. If the cat had died that morning, why was it still laying on her bed? Why hadn't Mrs M disposed of it?

Rita jumped around the kitchen, tears forming in her eyes.

"I don't want a dead cat on my bed," she protested.

Mrs M stopped what she was doing and turned, "now stop your fussing Rita, the cat was taken to the vets for disposal."

"But...?" Rita raced from the kitchen back to her bedroom. The cat was gone. There was no sign of it anywhere. Only the cushions and teddy bear lay in their usual places.

That night Rita lay in bed with a sense of relief. Flora was in the bedroom across the hall and the mangey black cat was dead. She turned over and pulled the covers around her neck, tucking herself neatly into place.

As she closed her eyes and nestled down to sleep, she felt the weight of something jump onto the bed, felt it pad across the covers and stop. Rita would have thought it was the cat had she not known of its demise. Nevertheless, she didn't want to find out, but curiosity compelled her.

She lifted her head slowly and turned it until she could see out of the corner of her left eye.

Oh my God, the black cat stared back at her, lifted its claws and struck.

Rita wrestled against the sharpness of each strike. Screaming and thrashing against the bedcovers until the starched white had turned crimson.

Why had Alexis and Katrina not come to her rescue? The truth was both slept deeply, unconsciously unaware of Rita's fate beside them.

It wasn't until the next morning that Rita was discovered.

She was alive, barely. Her eyes had been gauged from their sockets, her face disfigured by deep welts that rendered her almost unrecognisable.

Flora heard the commotion. She saw the ambulance take Rita away and heard the cries of Mrs M as she sobbed uncontrollably.

"Why ever would she do that?" cried Mrs M as she removed the bloody sheets from Rita's bed.

Mr M. was holding the knife, still dripping with remnants of Rita's blood.

"Clearly the child is disturbed," replied her husband. "She's very lucky to be alive."

"Is she though?" queried Mrs M. "She will be terribly disfigured and will never see again."

Flora heard their footsteps disappearing downstairs. She carried on stroking the black cat and smiled knowingly.

XXXVIII

Sister Ophelia arrived at the library just as Donal was about to take his break.

"Don't worry, Sister, I can take a break and help you at the same time," he comforted.

"Bless you," replied the nun. Donal was a kind young man, softly spoken with gentle demeanour. "This is not a book I have heard of, Sister, but that doesn't mean that it doesn't exist. I'll check the records."

Sister Ophelia waited patiently for Donal to return.

"The book is extremely rare, Sister. It's the only one of its kind in the world. I'm afraid our library would not be deemed worthy of housing such a treasure."

"Oh dear," sighed the nun, "thank you anyway, Donal."

Donal hadn't quite finished his sentence, "however, Sister," he interrupted, raising his tone slightly, "I do believe the Dean knows of its whereabouts."

Sister Ophelia spun on her heels. "The Dean at this university?" she enquired.

Donal nodded.

The nun wanted to kiss the young man's freckled cheek, but thought better of it. "Thank you, my child, thank you..." she cried.

Braden was correct the Coughing Donkey was indeed easy to find, not so much because of its infamous goat sign but mainly because it took pride of place in the centre of town.

Marley traced the sea of merry faces until she spotted Braden sitting in the farthest corner by the window.

He rose from his seat as she approached. "Glad you could make it. What can I get you to drink?"

"Just an orange juice please," replied Marley, removing her coat and making herself comfortable.

"How did the university visit go?" she asked as Braden returned with a tray of drinks and packets of crisps.

"Actually, it went well. I was lucky enough to meet the professor in person. He's just returned from a trip abroad."

"Does that mean you'll be hanging around for a while?" queried Marley with an inquisitive tone.

Braden nodded, "aye I suppose it does."

There was a look between them that Marley had never shared before. A butterfly moment when her legs felt weak and shaky and her heart pounded.

There was just one problem that she had yet to share. He knew she had a daughter out of wedlock, but she had never revealed Flora's age. Would Braden be disappointed when he found out that she had been a pregnant school girl? Would he think badly of her? Feel disgusted? Perhaps if she were to tell him the full story, the tranquilliser drug, the unconscious rape.

Tonight wasn't the right time. She would choose her moment carefully, get to know him a little better. For the time being, she was just another twenty something enjoying a drink with a newfound friend.

Sister Ophelia wrote a letter to the university, to Edward Trent, to be precise. She hadn't heard from the professor in a while. He had been travelling abroad, but she'd heard that he had recently returned. If anyone could help her unearth this book, he could, especially as this was his area of expertise?

She would wait for a reply and hoped it would be soon. Time was something she could not waste.

Marley said goodnight to Braden as they climbed the stairs to their separate rooms. She'd had an enjoyable night with lovely company.

She climbed into bed with a smile, recalling the silly conversations they had had and the bouts of laughter that had left her almost crying.

She turned out the light and nestled beneath the covers. Sleep was on the verge of claiming her when she heard a sound, a creak in the room as though something or someone were moving across the floor.

Marley reached for the lamp. There was no one there. It was just her imagination. The noises of an unfamiliar house. She left the light on anyway and drifted into sleep.

The following morning, she woke earlier than usual. The church bells were chiming in the distance and a glimmer of sunlight was poking through the curtains. She stretched and yawned. The lamp was still on.

"Silly me," she scolded herself, reaching for the switch. It was then that she noticed a trail of muddy footprints across the floor. They ended by the side of her bed. Marley threw back the covers to inspect the soles of her feet. They were clean. She jumped from the bed and placed her foot beside the muddy print. In comparison, her foot was much bigger. The imprint was the size of a younger person, a child.

Marley felt concerned. Should she inform Mrs Brightman? If she did and the woman assumed Marley had brought home a stranger, then she would be evicted from the boarding house. Instead, Marley set about cleaning the floor, removing all evidence of the muddy footprints and said nothing about it.

At breakfast, she found herself inspecting everyone's footwear. Mrs Brightman always wore slippers. Braden wore heavy leather walking boots and the new guest who had joined them recently wore brogues, all of a relatively much larger size than the prints left on her bedroom floor.

Marley shook the incident from her thoughts and turned them to the impending meeting she was about to have with her daughter Flora.

Marley took the bus to County Bottega. Her stomach churned as the vehicle rocked and swayed on the broken country road from town. Soon there was nothing but green fields and hills to look at. The scenery was quite spectacular and took her mind off the queazy feeling that mounted in her gut.

Finally, she reached her destination, descended from the bus, and waited. Minutes later, the social worker arrived and guided her to the Moreton's house.

Mr and Mrs Moreton were delightful people and Marley instantly admired their ability to care so lovingly for children who were not their own.

"It's lovely to meet you dear," announced Mrs M. "Flora will be home from school at any minute and I know she will be very excited."

Marley counted the minutes, entering into polite conversation as she waited patiently for Flora to make her appearance.

Suddenly, the wait was over and the front door flew open as a posse of school children entered the room. Marley searched the faces. She didn't need introducing to Flora, her child was obvious. The azure blue eyes, the bouncing golden curls. It was like looking into a mirror a decade ago.

"Here's your little angel," declared Mrs M, pulling Flora towards her for a huge hug. "Flora, this is your mammy."

Their eyes met. The little girl hesitated for a moment, then left Mrs M's embrace and flew into Marley's arms.

Marley lost herself in the warmth of the moment, nuzzling into Flora's soft curls, holding her tightly and stroking the baby soft skin she had so briefly experienced almost eight years ago. Tears flowed freely. She had not imagined such a wonderful reception.

Flora never left Marley's side for the next couple of hours. It was heartbreaking to have to say goodbye and leave her again.

"I'm coming back for you," promised Marley as she waved goodbye to the tear-stained face of Flora.

On the bus home Marley could think of no-one but Flora. She had not detected a speck of evil intent in the child. She was truly as angelic as Mrs Moreton had described. Marley's doubts about her parents' deaths dispersed. Flora wasn't capable of such atrocities.

XXXVIII

M arley couldn't hold back her excitement. She wanted Sister Ophelia to be the first to know how well her meeting with Flora had gone. After all, if the nun hadn't come looking for her, then she would never have known how to find Flora. She hurried to the convent.

"I'm sorry Sister Ophelia isn't here at the moment," answered Sister Grace. "Who shall I say called?"

Marley left her name and set off to find Braden, who she suspected was frequenting the Coughing Donkey.

Braden wasn't there. Marley went to the B&B, but he wasn't there either. Then she spotted him sitting on a bench overlooking the sea, eating fish and chips out of a newspaper. She approached, but he wasn't alone. A man was sitting beside him.

Marley stopped, rooted to the spot. She could feel pressure on her chest, as though someone or something was holding her back. The man was somehow significant, the shape of the back of his head, the way his hair was shaved to a point at the nape of his neck, the broadness of his shoulders.

Marley turned away, nausea engulfing her as she retched violently.

"Everything all right?" asked a familiar voice, as Sister Ophelia's hand patted her gently.

"Oh, Sister!" Marley embraced the nun fervently.

"You're trembling, child. What has happened?"

"The man on the bench, the one on the right," trembled Marley without looking back.

Sister Ophelia glanced in the direction. "There is only one man, my dear, and he's sitting on the left."

Marley found her strength and, through teary eyes, observed Braden sitting alone. She rushed towards him.

"Marley!" cried Braden.

Marley stared at him, eyes stinging, heart pounding. "Where did the other man go?" she pleaded.

Braden appeared shocked and threw aside his fish supper. "What man? Are you okay? Why are you so upset?"

"The man who was sitting next to you moments ago. Where is he?"

Braden glanced towards the nun questioningly, "there was no other man. I was alone."

If Braden were lying, then he was an accomplished expert. His performance was extremely convincing.

"Come now, sit down," demanded the nun. "You've got into quite a state."

"I really hate to leave you this way, but I have an appointment at the university," she declared.

"I'll take her back to the B&B. I'll look after her," promised Braden.

The nun nodded gratefully. "I shall check on you tomorrow."

Sister Ophelia hurried towards the university. Hopefully Donal would be there to meet her with news of the book.

He was going to contact the Dean's office and ask permission for Sister Ophelia to view it.

"I'm meeting Donal," declared Sister Ophelia to the solitary girl, who sat reading alone.

"Oh, Donal called in sick, but he left a note for you," replied the girl, glancing over silver framed glasses.

Sister Ophelia thanked her and read the note. Donal apologised for not having yet made contact with the Dean but assured her that he would do so on his return to work.

The nun's thoughts turned to those of Edward Trent, who had not replied to her last letter. Perhaps he had been busy. Perhaps he had headed off on another adventure.

The nun was just about the leave the library empty handed and frustrated when who should walk through the door at the exact time, but none other than Edward Trent himself.

"Sister!" he cried with a tone of excitement.

"Edward, I thought you were avoiding me?"

Edward seemed perplexed. "Why would you think that?" he pleaded.

"You haven't replied to my letter," answered the nun.

"My dear Sister, I can assure you I have received no such letter." The professor was exceedingly apologetic. "Perhaps it is lying in my post tray, unopened. I have only recently returned from India.

Please follow me to my study. I must rectify this misdemeanour at once."

Sister Ophelia followed Edward down a labyrinth of corridors.

"This is my very own oasis," he declared, offering her a seat and fixing a tray of refreshments.

"Oh Edward, you lead such an exciting life. Look at all these artefacts. You must have travelled the world. You shall have to change your name to Phileas Fogg if this continues," taunted the nun.

The professor chuckled as he poured tea and took a seat behind his desk.

"Now the matter of your letter, let me see..." he flicked through a mountain of unopened mail that sat precariously in a tray on one side of his enormous mahogany bureau, "ha, here it is I would recognise that handwriting anywhere."

Sister Ophelia sipped at her tea as Edward Trent proceeded to deal with her missing letter.

The room went quiet. Only the sound of the professor's breathing could be heard. He was studying the letter intensely, his expression indescribable, his brow furrowed, the unkindness of age more defined than ever before.

"Is everything all right?" begged the nun.

Edward looked towards her. For a solitary moment, the man she had first met at her sister's wake appeared to have disappeared. There was almost a darkness in the face that stared back at her, a darkness that sent a cold shiver racing through her body.

The professor immediately remembered himself and smiled. "Of course, Sister. I am stunned that you have knowledge of such a book. Tell me how you do so?"

Sister Ophelia would not betray Father Ignatius' confession.

"I was attending to the late father's belongings, and I happened upon the title of that book. I was merely interested in understanding its significance to Catholicism and why he would have knowledge of such a title."

The nun felt for her rosary and clutched it tightly. She hoped God would forgive her deceit.

"Yes, it is rather curious that a Catholic priest should pursue a book which denies the very existence of his belief."

"I couldn't comment," replied Sister Ophelia. "I myself have no knowledge of its contents."

The professor relaxed. Whatever had plagued his thoughts previously had, for the moment, dispelled.

"This is not a book for you, Sister. It speaks of the occult, of demons, of the destruction of the world."

"I see, still I am curious to look upon it. You have seen it yourself?"

"It is merely touched upon in the study of parapsychology and the paranormal. Only briefly, you understand. There is only one of its kind, therefore, it is treated with extreme fragility. Should it ever be lost or destroyed, it would be catastrophic to such teachings. It is to the occultist what the Bible is to the Christian."

"It is written by prophets, disciples?" queried the nun.

The professor sighed deeply, the width of his broad shoulders expanding beneath the weight of his despair.

"My dear Sister, this book is written by Satan himself."

"I see," pondered the nun, "but it does live here in this university?"

Edward nodded.

"Could I see it?"

Edward hesitated, "you want to see it, even after what I just told you?"

"I want to see what the opposition looks like, if that makes sense?" smiled Sister Ophelia with a tone of determination.

"I should have to clear it with the Dean. It's kept in the university vault," explained the professor.

"Then please go ahead. You have quenched my curiosity," replied the nun.

The gaze between them intensified, each holding the other to account. It was Edward who looked away first. "Give me a couple of days. I'll be in touch."

Sister Ophelia left the university with a heavy heart. She had located the book, but retrieving its contents appeared almost impossible. If, as Edward said, it was locked in a vault, then how would she be able to take a look inside?

Father Ignatius' letter had stated that the way to kill the demon lay within its pages, specifically chapter 13. Edward Trent appeared possessive of the book. Was it because the book didn't exist at all and he was stalling for time, or was there another explanation? She had witnessed his expression when he read her letter and the cautiousness of his answers about the book. Was Edward Trent harbouring a secret?

XXXIX

The following morning, Sister Ophelia paid a visit to the Beachcombers B&B.

"Morning, Sister, please come in," greeted Mrs Brightman, almost curtseying at the sight of the nun. "What can I do for you? Would you be wanting some refreshments?"

Sister Ophelia declined politely. "I'm looking for Marley?"

Mrs Brightman's broad smile vanished as she pointed towards the dining room. "She's in there."

Marley and Braden were breakfasting together, clearly an activity Mrs Brightman disapproved of.

Marley looked fragile and pale. Sleep had not visited her the night before, but her face brightened at the sight of Sister Ophelia.

"How are you feeling?" questioned the nun, though she was certain she already knew the answer.

"I'm alright. Sorry about the performance yesterday, I feel such a fool. I must have imagined the other man." Marley didn't believe her own words, nor did the nun, but Braden assured her he had sat alone the entire time.

Braden pulled out a chair for the sister and poured her a cup of tea.

"Marley has spoken about you a lot, Sister. It's nice to actually meet you," he said.

Sister Ophelia couldn't say the same about Braden. Until last evening Marley had not spoken of him at all, but she smiled sedately, replying, "and you too."

The young man's face seemed familiar, though the nun had no idea why.

There was music playing softly in the background of the dining room, a sporadic static whistle, the accompanying feature of a radio. As the music stopped, the lilt of a young man's voice echoed across the room as he announced the news.

Sister Ophelia wasn't particularly listening until she heard a familiar name.

And finally, the body of a young man has been found on the grounds of the university this morning. The man has been identified as Donal Riordan, aged twenty-two. Foul play is not suspected and the cause of death is confirmed as suicide.

"Sister, are you alright?" queried Marley. "You've gone awfully pale."

The nun nodded. She was just about to explain the reason for her sudden pallor when Braden interrupted.

"There's no way Donal would kill himself!" he declared, outwardly upset. "I don't believe that for a minute."

"You knew Donal?" questioned the sister.

Braden nodded, "we grew up together. Next-door neighbours, same schools, our mams were friends. It was Donal who suggested I visit the university, who praised the professor. I can't believe he's dead."

Marley called for more tea. It was a moment that required it.

"How did you know Donal?" enquired Braden, pouring a second cup.

"He helped me with some information. He was so patient and kind. I was supposed to meet him yesterday, but was told he was taken sick," answered the nun.

"You visited the university yesterday?"

"Yes," replied the nun. "Donal was procuring a specific book for me via the Dean."

"I must let me mam know," proffered Braden, changing the subject, "I better head home later."

Marley nodded sympathetically. She knew home for Braden was on the other side of the island, just as it had been for her. She knew Braden wouldn't be back until the next day.

"What book were you looking for?" queried Marley as Braden headed for the door.

"Oh, it's very rare. Kept in the vault, I'm told. Only viewable at the Dean's approval."

"The Philosophy of Demons!" blurted Braden, stopping in his tracks.

"You know it?" pleaded the nun.

Braden nodded, "it's a massive part of our study into occultism."

"That's what you study?" asked the sister.

"Well, it's part of the curriculum," replied Braden. "A very interesting part, too."

"How so?" asked the nun, intrigued.

"The Philosophy of Demons is supposedly written by Satan himself," Braden shrugged. "It's his blueprint to takeover the Christian world, wipe out all denominations and replace it with the one true faith, Satanism."

"Do you believe it's possible?" asked Sister Ophelia.

"Anything is possible, Sister, in the right hands!"

The answer was haunting. World domination had been achieved before, Hitler being a prime example. Fortunately, he didn't succeed, not that someone else could.

Braden excused himself. "I'll need to pack a bag. Hopefully, see you tomorrow."

He was about to leave the room again when he turned back and paused. "Sister, the book isn't kept in a vault. It's kept in a safe in the professor's study."

A chill coasted Sister Ophelia's body, the hair on her neck stood to attention. She was about to ask the name of the professor, but she was certain she already knew it.

As Braden left for home, Marley confided in the nun.

"Please don't think me crazy, Sister, but I've been having a weird experience," she began.

After the events of the last few months, the nun was well versed in the word 'weird'. She knew that whatever Marley was about to say would no longer shock her.

"Care to elaborate Marley?"

Marley spoke of unexplained small, muddy footprints appearing across the carpet of her bedroom. It happened on each night that she spent at the B&B and she couldn't explain it.

"Your door is locked? The footprints are not your own? They appear at night?" quizzed the nun.

Marley nodded.

"At first I thought someone was entering my room, but it's impossible to unlock a door when the key that locked it is still in the other side. The windows are always closed, and it's a long way down to the ground below. I can't imagine anyone could scale the height of the wall without a ladder."

The nun paused, remembering the muddy footprints she had found outside her bedroom door at Orla's house. Footprints left by the deceased Amelia.

"What is it, Sister?" begged Marley, observing the sombre expression on the nun's face.

Sister Ophelia turned to her. "Perhaps you are being visited by a spirit!"

"A ghost!" exclaimed Marley.

"An entity," replied the nun, "probably someone close to you."

"I don't like the sound of that at all," shuddered Marley.

"You say the footprints are small, befitting a child, not an adult?"

Marley nodded.

"That would rule out your parents," pondered Sister Ophelia. "You have a sibling?"

"I had a sister, Niamh."

"She was a child when she died?"

"Err... thirteen, but she was small for her age. She had an illness. I don't remember the name."

The nun sighed. "I think she may be your mysterious visitor."

Marley was stunned. How was it possible for her younger sister, who died years before, to suddenly be visiting her in the middle of the night?

"You think that's possible?" she challenged.

"I know it is!" declared the nun. "I have firsthand experience myself."

"Then what does it mean, Sister?"

There was no easy way to say it, "you could be in danger Marley!"

XL

Flora was dressed in her best clothes, blue lace dress decorated with a large white bow and black shoes. She was only allowed to wear them on special occasions and today she was spending alone time with her mammy, comprising a visit to the park and a picnic feast courtesy of Mrs Moreton.

The hands on the clock didn't turn fast enough for Flora's liking. She felt excited and impatient.

The hours passed, but mammy didn't arrive.

She watched the disgruntled expressions on the Moreton's faces turn to sympathy. What did it mean? Was her mammy not coming?

Suddenly, there was a knock at the door. It wasn't her mammy, but the social worker.

She heard remnants of a mumbled conversation, then saw the flushed face of Mrs M appear round the door.

"Your mammy missed the bus, Flora. She's terribly sorry, but she'll be here tomorrow instead."

Flora felt despondent as she changed out of her pretty dress and kicked off the shiny black shoes.

Had her mammy really missed the bus, or was it just an excuse because she had changed her mind? Did she know about Flora's dark shadow? Was that the reason for not attending the appointment?

Flora's head spun with questions, weaving an enormous web of uncertainty.

She ran to Mrs Moreton's bedroom and grabbed the Bible again. She held it tight until it turned a fiery red. She didn't want to let it go, but something, someone was telling her to. She wanted it to burn her hands. To transfer its goodness into her, even if it meant burning the flesh from her bones.

The heat seared until Flora had no choice but to drop it. It hit the ground and immediately extinguished. Flora's palm was stinging. She unfolded her fingers. The imprint of a cross was glowing upon it, branded into the skin, blistering and swollen. For a moment Flora smiled. God had not forsaken her. His mark lay across her palm. She was good, after all, but Flora hadn't realised that the cross she bore was inverted. The mark did not belong to God, but to the Devil!

Marley could hardly forgive herself for abandoning Flora at such short notice. She knew the child would be devastated, but she had to get to the bottom of the haunting footsteps, otherwise she could not ensure Flora's safety or her own.

She travelled beside Sister Ophelia on the bus to Ballykilne. Their words were few, both focused on the significance of the journey and its importance.

They walked the half mile into the village. The remnants of a charred house and church greeting them. Marley stopped. "I don't think I can go any further," she declared.

Sister Ophelia linked her arm. "Of course you can child, God walks beside us on this mission. You must keep faith."

The graveyard had been spared destruction. Wooden debris plagued the scorched earth around its perimeter, but the headstones were intact.

Niamh Sutton's headstone was easy to find standing closest to the where the church doors once opened. It had been chosen for that very reason so that her father had a clear view of her every time he entered and departed the church.

The earth had been disturbed, mostly by the trample of firefighters as they struggled to control the blaze.

In the distance, a lone man was digging at the earth, no doubt preparing the ground for the next deceased soul. He stood and removed his cap, towelling away the sweat of his actions with soiled fingers.

"Can I help you?" he called.

Sister Ophelia waved him towards them.

"Is there something I can do for you?" asked the man as he approached.

"Are you the gravedigger?" questioned the nun sympathetically.

"Indeed, I am, Sister. The one and only. Been burying these villagers for the last thirty years."

"Have any of the graves been disturbed recently?" she asked, knowing the question to be obscure.

The man scratched at his head with dirt encrusted finger nails. "Not to my knowledge. There was some disturbance when the firemen were here, but mostly the graves have been untouched."

The nun looked down at the headstone of Niamh Sutton.

"Poor wee child," added the man, "she doesn't normally get visitors now her parents have gone."

"I suppose we all get forgotten eventually," replied Sister Ophelia.

The man sniffed, the hint of a smile crossing his lips, "she'll never be forgotten Sister, not now."

The gesture appeared kind, but with a hint of sarcasm. "And why's that?" questioned the nun.

"She haunts this graveyard," declared the man, "every night since her parents' death. No one comes here after dark, no one dare."

"You've seen her?"

The man shook his head. "I'm pleased to say I have not and I never want to either. If she locks eyes with you, you've had it!"

The man sliced a grubby finger across his throat.

Sister Ophelia shook her head and sighed. "Superstitious nonsense."

"You ask the relatives of people who've died if it's just superstition, they'll tell you. You see Niamh and she sees you, then you get a visit from her. Muddy footprints across your bedroom floor. Next minute you're a gonna!"

Marley flinched at the reference to muddy footprints, as a chill coasted her spine.

"You related?" questioned the man, suddenly taking notice of her.

Marley shook her head.

"We're just visiting," thanked the nun. "Heard about the tragedy and wanted to pay our respects."

"It's going to be dark soon. You best make sure you're not around when it is," warned the man, sauntering away.

"What do we do now, Sister?" asked Marley nervously as they left the graveyard.

"Well, as I see it, we have two choices, child. We wait for Niamh to appear or we go home!"

Marley knew which she would rather, but then she would go home empty-handed without the answers she sought.

"Let's dine at the public house, wait until it goes dark, then come back," suggested the nun.

As they sat picking at beef stew and dumplings, it felt as though they were consuming their last supper.

"Now I know what death row feels like," remarked Marley, burping loudly from the over zealous ingestion of cider.

Sister Ophelia summoned a smile. She did not know what awaited them or whether they would live through the night, but she did know that unless she put an end to Niamh Sutton, Marley may not live to see another day.

The shadows of darkness cast its gloom across Ballykilne. The brightness of a full moon retreated behind the weight of threatening rain clouds and stars hid from view.

As drops of rain threatened, they headed back to the graveyard. The night was chilly; the wind howling through the charred timbers of the wounded church. The cemetery was still.

Marley gripped the nun's arm tightly, searching the area for a sighting of Niamh.

"Have you done this before?" whispered Marley.

"Hundreds of times!" added the nun.

"Really?"

"No Marley, never!" came the reply.

"Then what are you going to do when we find her?" dithered Marley, who couldn't stop herself from shaking. Whether it was the cold of the wind or the fear that raged through her body, she wasn't certain.

"I have Father Ignatius' book of exorcism, my Bible, my rosary, some holy water and my faith," replied the nun.

"Is that it?"

"Unless you know of anything else that might help, then yes!" muttered Sister Ophelia.

"What about a wooden stake?"

"We're not hunting vampires, Marley," replied the nun wryly.

A hint of movement caught their attention. A lone figure floating between the gravestones. A child.

"It's coming towards us, Sister."

The nun clutched at her rosary as the figure moved closer.

A girl, or rather the remains of her, hovered before them. Feathered flesh hung from exposed bone. Shades of necrosis painted her skin blue and purple. The clothes she had worn at her burial, disintegrating. Strands of blond hair now the colour of the earth.

"Niamh?" Marley spoke her name with compassion. It was difficult to be certain the figure was her sister, given the state of decomposition, but she recognised the heart-shaped silver necklace that dangled from her scrawny neck. It had once belonged to their grandmother.

The figure tilted its head to one side as though the word were once recognisable.

Marley stepped forward.

"Careful, you might think that's your sister, but I assure it isn't," advised the nun.

Marley stopped dead. "Who is she then?"

SEE BELOW

"Not who, but what," replied Sister Ophelia. "A demon has taken up residence in the sister you once knew. Now get behind me."

Marley took refuge, sticking so close she was almost velcroed to the sister's clothing.

The demon hadn't moved, the blackness of its eyes fixed upon its opposition.

Sister Ophelia raised her crucifix and began to recite the exorcism prayer. She had found it amongst the pages of Father Ignatius' diary, an object she retrieved at the same time as the red binder. It bore a warning:

To be said by a priest only,
by the Order of His Holiness
Pope Leo XIII.

Sister Ophelia couldn't worry about that now. She was standing face to face with a demon.

"Holy water!" she demanded, "right pocket."

Marley fished for it, unscrewed the lid. "What now?"

"Get ready, when I say douse the creature with it."

Marley was breathing heavily, nervously panting to procure the oxygen she so desperately sought.

Sister Ophelia, whose outward calm and control cut a fearless figure, though the nun was actually feeling quite the opposite inside. Her heart was beating so fast she thought at any moment it might stop.

At this point, the demon had risen upwards and was hovering above them.

"Recite the Lord's prayer," demanded the nun.

Marley began.

"Louder Marley, it has to hear you."

Marley was almost shouting now, fighting to make herself heard against a fierce wind that whipped against them. Her voice drowning beneath the sharpness of its icy blasts.

The demon glanced towards her, "whore, prostitute, heathen, harlot," the words sprayed from its mouth like venom. The voice was malevolent, unholy. It echoed through Marley's soul with a vengeance.

Marley's voice began to weaken.

"Ignore it. It wants to upset you, it wants you to give in. Fight Marley, your life depends on it," cried Sister Ophelia as she wrestled to keep them both alive.

The Lord's prayer roared from Marley's lips as she held the demon with her gaze.

It laughed maniacally, but Marley did not falter.

"Any minute now," declared the nun reciting the final sentence to cast out the demon, "throw it now!" she screamed.

A spray of holy water made contact with the beast. It let out a blood-curdling scream, writhing and snarling with pain. Its eyes glowed red as it lunged towards them.

Marley and Sister Ophelia held each other tightly and closed their eyes. This was it, the moment that could change everything.

Suddenly the wind dropped, the air warmed, and the night became still once again. The demon had disappeared.

"You did it!" screamed Marley, releasing her grip on the sister.

"We did it," replied the nun. "I couldn't have done it without you."

XLI

It was the day of Donal Riordan's funeral. Braden had returned to the B&B. Marley and Sister Ophelia were still reeling from their experience in Ballykilne, but Donal deserved their attention.

Marley, not having personally met the young man, was merely there as a means of support.

The service was to take place in the Abbey of St. Catharines that afternoon.

Students and masters from the university filled a proportion of its seating. A small group of Donal's family and friends huddled together on the front pews as Marley and Braden slotted into seating close to the exit.

Sister Ophelia took her place amongst the nuns.

The service had just begun when the door of the old church opened.

The sound of brisk footsteps echoed through the silence, the tapping of heels kissing the hard stone floor beneath.

A sudden coldness enveloped Marley, and she shuddered, hugging at her coat for warmth. The feeling was momentary, occurring only as the late comer passed beside her.

She glanced upwards in time to see the outline of a tall man disappearing down the aisle. Nausea swept over her, followed by an encompassing feeling of dread.

"You all right?" asked Braden as Marley fidgeted beside him.

Marley nodded.

"You look terribly pale," whispered Braden. "Shall we leave?"

Marley shook her head. If Braden had any inkling of the night she had faced with Sister Ophelia, he might have forgiven her absence today, but as he did not, Marley was determined that he pay his respects and would not allow Donal's funeral to become about her.

As the congregation flowed from the church and into the graveyard, Marley's thoughts were drawn to the memory of the night before. She searched the sea of faces for Sister Ophelia.

The nun didn't look too well, either, but she smiled and nodded in Marley's direction.

"Did you notice the latecomer, the man with the noisy shoes?" asked Marley as they strolled towards the open burial plot that was to become Donal's final resting place.

"Yeah, that's the professor," replied Braden, directing Marley towards the graveside.

Marley was certain the professor and the man she had witnessed sitting beside Braden on the bench that evening were one and the same.

The committal began.

A lone soprano caressed the moment with a rendition of Amazing Grace, as Donal's coffin was lowered into place.

"So final don't you think?" muttered Braden.

"If you don't believe," replied Marley.

"And if I did believe, how does that make it different?"

"Because then death is only the beginning!"

The service was over. Guests scattered randomly, heading in the direction of the function room at the rear of the Coughing Donkey, where a feast had been laid out.

Braden was eager to leave, but Marley had spotted the professor deep in conversation with Donal's parents, his profile shaded behind the branches of an overgrown tree.

"Why don't you go and secure a table for us?" suggested Marley.

"You're not coming?" frowned Braden.

"To be sure I am, just need a word with Sister Ophelia."

Braden accepted the lie and sauntered toward the public house.

Marley couldn't help but stare at the professor and the more she did, the more disturbed she felt.

It was the same feeling she had experienced when Braden was eating fish and chips on the bench overlooking the sea. He swore he dined alone the entire time and that at no point had anyone joined him. Could Marley believe him?

The professor was moving now, not heading towards the public house, but in the direction of the university.

Marley hurried behind him, keeping just enough distance so as not to be noticed.

Braden would wonder where she had got to, so she mustn't take too long, but she needed to find out for herself.

As the man reached the gates of the university, he paused to light a cigarette. Marley took refuge beside the nearest building and waited. If she dallied for too long, the man would disappear and she would miss her chance. On the other hand, if he saw her, then she would have a lot of explaining to do.

Marley summoned the courage and threw an anxious glance toward the gateway. The man was still there, stubbing out the tobacco with the heel of his shoe. He disappeared through the gates, heading toward the library building.

Marley kept pace, throwing herself behind the nearest bush as the man turned suddenly before disappearing inside.

Marley crossed the paved courtyard and up the steps to the library entrance. She pulled open the door and stepped inside. There was nothing but silence in the empty corridors of the building.

Nausea mounted inside her as she removed her kitten heels and padded towards the nearest open door.

She heard movement inside. The sound of a telephone dialling and the legs of a wooden chair scraping across the floor. Then his voice. A voice she could never forget. Marley froze. She didn't need to see his face now. She knew exactly who he was.

XLII

Today was about Flora. Quality time spent with her daughter. Marley arrived on time with a pink teddy bear and a bag of sweets.

Flora was waiting.

"You came!" she cried as Mrs M opened the door.

Marley opened her arms. "Of course I did, and I'm so very sorry about the other day. I wanted to be here, really I did."

It was a pretty day, sunny and bright. Birds were singing and the first buds of spring were beginning to bloom as they set off toward the park.

Flora rode the swing, the see-saw and the slide, repeating the circuit six or seven times. Marley looked on with a smile.

"It's my birthday next week," shouted Flora, "I'll be eight."

"Perhaps you should have a party," replied Marley enthusiastically. "Presents and a cake, jelly and ice cream."

"Candles and fairy lights," added Flora.

"I'll speak to Mrs M later about it."

Flora hopped and skipped across the lawned area and headed towards the duck pond.

"Careful at the edge," warned Marley. "Don't want you falling into the water."

"Don't you think it's amazing how ducks just sit on the water and don't drown?" began Flora.

"Well, I suppose they're specially made for the water. Their feet are like paddles and their feathers are waterproof."

"Who do you think made them?" questioned Flora philosophically.

"Why God, of course," replied Marley without hesitation.

Flora studied her mammy for a moment, "how can you be sure that God made them?"

"It says so in the Bible."

"Does it?"

Marley wrestled to bring the verse to mind, "Colossians 1: 16-17," she recited.

"How do you know so much about the Bible?" continued Flora.

"Probably because my father was a vicar. Reading the Bible was a part of my life, just like saying prayers."

Flora nodded, remembering the old vicar with whom she had spent a short and traumatic amount of time.

"Shall we sit here and have our picnic? You can watch the ducks at the same time," suggested Marley.

She unpacked a chequered rug and set out sandwiches, homemade cake slices, biscuits, fruit and lemonade.

Flora munched her way steadily through the treats.

"I don't think God likes me!" she declared thoughtfully.

Marley was taken aback by the sentence, "of course he does Flora, God loves everyone."

"He doesn't love me," she shook her head defiantly.

"Why would you think that?"

"He did this to me when I was holding the Bible."

Flora uncurled her fingers, displaying a scabby red mark. Marley looked closer. The imprint was of an upside down crucifix seared into the palm of her hand. Marley tried not to outwardly react, even though everything inside her was screaming with terror.

"That looks sore Flora, have you been playing with matches?"

Flora shook her head, "it was Mrs Moreton's Bible. I picked it up and it burst into flames."

Marley could feel herself shaking now. She had to stay in control. She couldn't let Flora witness her distress. Her mind was racing as snippets of conversations with Sister Ophelia returned to her memory. The ones describing Flora as having an ability, although probably not God given.

If she'd had previous doubts, then they had just been dispelled. She'd wondered at Flora's involvement with her parents' deaths, but always dismissed it without substance. Suddenly that question was returning, and she feared the answer was a resounding, 'yes.'

"Perhaps it's time to go," she declared hurriedly, packing away the empty containers and folding the rug.

"So soon?" complained Flora.

"I'm sure I felt a spot of rain," replied Marley, even though not a cloud interrupted the pale blue canvas of sky and the sun hadn't stopped shining.

"Do you think I'm good?" began Flora, skipping alongside, her small fingers wrapped around Marley's hand.

"Yes... of course I do, why don't you?" replied Marley, almost afraid of the answer.

"I think I am, but then sometimes I think I'm bad."

"We all have a little of each in us," declared Marley, quickening the pace.

"I try to be good, but something that lives inside me tells me to be bad. I try not to listen, but it makes me."

Marley was picking up speed, dashing in front of moving cars to cross the street, taking any shortcut that would save them time, however dangerous.

Then came the ultimate confession, "I didn't mean to hurt your parents."

Marley stopped dead, pulling Flora towards her. The blue of the child's eyes were glazed with tears as her bottom lip trembled uncontrollably.

"What happened Flora, tell me," begged Marley, gripping the child by the shoulders.

Flora was sobbing now, tears flowing freely down both cheeks.

Marley was overcome by compassion and hugged her child closely. "It's okay, it's okay," she declared softly.

The voice that followed did not belong to a little girl.

It was the voice that had echoed from the depths of the demon two nights earlier. Her daughter, like her sister, was merely a vessel, a puppet played by an uncontrollable force.

Marley pulled the child away from her.

She stared into the depth of her eyes. The paleness of blue overcome by darkness. Flora's mouth was agape, but unmoving.

"I killed your parents!" roared the voice with malignancy.

It was a surreal moment as though time had frozen and Marley was the only person on earth who could hear the indignant tones of the demonic force. Everyone around her was going about their business, blissfully unaware of the evil presence that controlled her daughter.

Marley was suddenly back in the moment. Flora skipping beside her, eyes as blue as the ocean. The voice obscured her thoughts as she struggled to collect herself.

"What's wrong mammy?" asked the sweet, gentle voice of her daughter.

"Nothing Flora, mammy's just tired that's all."

It was a relief to hand Flora over to Mrs M. and be riding the bus home again, much to the foster mother's surprise.

Flora, fortunately, had no recollection of what had happened, but Marley was not so lucky.

In her haste to retreat from the Moreton's home, she had neglected to mention Flora's birthday party. She would make contact in a day or so, when the memory of her daughter's inhuman baritone was fading from her thoughts.

Marley was certain that Flora and the man she had followed to the university library were connected. She knew that danger lay ahead. She must warn Sister Ophelia at once.

XLIII

Sister Ophelia headed back to the library. She knew that Edward Trent had been lying about the satanic book. Braden had confirmed it. It lay somewhere in his study and the nun wanted to find it.

The library was quiet. Edward wasn't there. She followed the corridor to his study and knocked.

Only silence answered. She knocked again.

The door was unlocked. She turned it cautiously and peered inside. "Edward?" she called, but he didn't reply.

Closing the door behind her, Sister Ophelia searched the contents of Edward Trent's desk. She scoured his book shelves and flipped through the contents of his coffee table, but the book wasn't there.

The nun stood perplexed, studying the mahogany panelling that lined the room. The university was old, this part more so. Perhaps, as at the convent, there was a priest hole behind one of the panels. A secret hiding place built into centuries old houses where priests would secret themselves to avoid persecution.

She started tapping on the wood, listening for a discrepancy in the sound and pulling ornate candlesticks that adorned the walls, but no hidden passageway revealed itself. She hurried to the fireplace and pushed at the bricks with an iron poker resting beside the ashes.

Nothing, nothing and then a brick dislodged as one half of the fireplace moved slowly aside, revealing the entrance to a passageway behind it.

Sister Ophelia bent forward and stepped cautiously into the mouth of darkness. A rush of cool air greeting her as she entered. The nun steadied herself, feeling disoriented and vulnerable. The passageway was wide, cavernous, much more than the dimensions of a simple priest's hole. The nun's eyes struggled to adjust to the depth of oblivion that stretched before her.

Blinded by the absence of light, she eased herself along a damp and slippy path, using her fingers to trace the wall of the passageway one jagged stone at a time. One incorrect step and she would crash to the stone floor beneath.

She continued her journey, creeping through the darkness, muttering to Father Ignatius for availing her of such a task. Step after step, fingertips searching, footsteps timidly feeling the path beneath them, praying for a shaft of light to enhance her journey.

Perhaps the end was in sight. The stone wall had ended and there was the hint of something flickering in the distance.

The nun pushed forward bravely.

A moment later, candles were welcoming her into the broadness of a large room roughly carved into the rock bed beneath the university. She blinked awkwardly, adjusting her eyes to the newfound light.

She glanced around. Was she alone?

"Sister," she heard the familiar tone of Edward Trent's voice call to her from the shadows, "please don't be shy, come in, come in, though you are a trifle early."

The nun moved forward until the figure of the enigmatic professor became visible.

"I assume you're looking for this?" he beckoned her towards him.

Perched upon a wooden pedestal was a leather-bound book, scarred and disfigured, presumably by age. It bore the title she had been searching for.

"Touch it," ordered the professor.

The nun hesitated. The book was grotesque enough to look upon. She wasn't sure she wanted to touch it.

"Go ahead, Sister, what are you waiting for?" demanded the professor.

Sister Ophelia placed a single finger on the rough, gnarled surface of the book and prodded. It indented at her touch, engorged and bloated like skin, as a swell of dark red blood erupted to the surface and oozed freely. She pulled herself away.

"This cannot be the book I am seeking," she declared with scepticism.

"I can assure you it is," replied Edward, "and this is the blood of Satan." He wiped a lone finger across the red liquid and dabbed it onto his tongue.

Sister Ophelia realised that Edward Trent was not all he had first appeared. She scoured the shadows for confirmation. Etched into the stonework were symbols and images that she recognised immediately. The professor was a devil worshipper.

"Surprise!" he declared as the dawn of realisation appeared on the nun's expression.

Her mind was racing. The interest he had shown in Flora. The fictitious offers of help. Like a jigsaw puzzle, the pieces were falling into place.

The nun searched for an exit, but the room was enclosed. She raced towards the darkened passage that had led her here, but his hands were upon her, strong and restrictive.

"Please, Sister, show a little dignity," he yelled as she kicked and punched herself to freedom, but her strength was no match for that of the professor. He launched her into the air and everything went black.

XLIV

Marley jumped from the bus and ran towards the convent, but Sister Ophelia was not at home and Sister Grace did not know where she had gone or when she would return.

Marley headed back to the B&B. She knocked on Braden's door and waited.

"Come in. How was the picnic?" gushed Braden with enthusiasm, but Marley had no time for small talk as she gasped for breath.

"Sit down. What's wrong?" he queried.

Marley sighed heavily.

"I need your help," she confessed, "but first there's something I must tell you. If at the end of it you want me to leave you alone, then I will, but please believe me when I tell you that what I am about to reveal is the truth and nothing but the truth."

Marley recounted her ordeal of almost eight years earlier, leaving no detail untold. If there was a chance of a relationship with Braden, and she hoped that there was, then she wanted no hidden secrets between them.

Braden listened. His eyes were wide with disbelief, his expression alternating between that of horror and confusion.

Marley finished her story and waited. Braden said nothing. He paced the floor, deep in thought.

Perhaps she had scared him away, but at least she had been honest.

Braden hadn't uttered a word to her for the last ten minutes. She headed for the door. It was obvious what Braden was thinking.

Suddenly, she felt the warmth of his hand close over hers as he pulled her towards him and hugged her tightly. There were no words between them. The embrace was enough to answer all of her questions.

Braden brushed her hair to one side gently and said, "now tell me what you need me to do?"

There was a knock at the door and Mrs Brightman's voice bellowed, "what are you two up to? I'll have no shenanigans in my establishment."

Braden crossed to the door, "we're just talking Mrs B, see both fully clothed!" he declared as the landlady almost tripped across the threshold.

"Make sure that's all it is," she scolded. "If you want supper, you better come downstairs. I don't do room service."

In a corner of the dining room, Marley and Braden whispered closely.

"I want to know everything I can about the professor," she announced.

"That shouldn't be too difficult," advised Braden. "He used to work at a different university and I have a friend there who will be able to help us."

"Excellent. First thing tomorrow, we must go and see him," declared Marley.

Sister Ophelia was regaining consciousness. Her vision was blurry and the pain that raged inside her head did nothing to quell the memory of her predicament.

She scoured the room, blinking through the candlelight in search of the malign professor, but Edward Trent had disappeared, leaving the nun bound and gagged in his secret room.

The candles were extinguishing slowly. Only the glow of three half melted church candles provided the source of light. The nun did not know her fate, but she knew that the fate of many lay in her hands. She needed the book if she were to execute Father Ignatius' parting words.

She searched the room for something, anything, that would release her bindings. The nun sighed, at times like this she would caress her rosary and pray, but it was out of reach. Hanging majestically from her neck, whilst her hands were tied firmly behind the chair.

"Think," scolded the nun inwardly, spying the edge of the crucifix dangling on her lap. She bounced the chair ferociously until the crucifix took flight and looped over her shoulder, landing against her back within touching distance of her fingers.

Sister Ophelia sighed heavily with frustration. What had that exercise achieved, except for changing the position of her rosary? She closed her eyes, "if ever I needed your help Lord, it has to be now," she prayed.

Her fingers wrestled to touch the rosary, something stabbed at her skin, something that had never happened before. She wriggled and squirmed beneath her confines, clasping the edge of the crucifix, where the sharpness pierced her skin again. Perhaps it had been damaged by the brutish behaviour of Edward Trent.

She traced the cross with her fingertips. The wood had splintered, leaving a knife edge at the base of the effigy. Sister Ophelia wasted no time utilising the severity of the cross and set to work sawing at the binding around her wrists. It was no easy task and excruciatingly painful, as her distorted position on the chair tugged at her muscles with ferocity.

The third candle burned out, and the bindings were still in place. The nun worked feverishly until, finally, her wrists dropped to freedom. She untied her ankles and rose cautiously, her head spinning uncontrollably and her vision momentarily unreliable.

She steadied herself by using the chair as an aid and made her way towards the book. She tucked it inside her habit, trying desperately not to squeeze it as blood began to seep from its binding and leak onto her under garment. She retrieved a candle from the floor and used it to guide herself back along the passage.

XLV

Castle Craig was a small village on the outskirts of the capital. Known for its idyllic panoramas, infamous university and historic castles. Built in the 1700s, the community had lived through war, plague, famine and tyranny. It was a place steeped in history, and had become one of Ireland's most popular tourist destinations.

"Isn't this just lovely?" admired Marley as she descended the bus.

"Unbelievably pretty," added Braden, unfolding a map of the area and studying it closely.

"I think the university is this way," he directed, grabbing Marley by the hand and taking charge.

The village was no more than four miles in diameter, which meant finding the university was easy.

Stopping at a telephone box just outside the gates, Braden dialled his friend.

"No worries Mickey," he said, replacing the receiver with a smile.

"Well?" questioned Marley.

"He's on his way to meet to us now."

Mickey Feenan was a well built, broad shouldered, athletic looking chap with a mop of prematurely grey hair and a bright red beard.

He shook hands and smiled cheerily. "What brings you to my neck of the woods?" he enquired.

"I'm looking for some information on Professor T," replied Braden.

That was the first time Marley had heard him add a letter to the end of the tutor's name. She shuddered uncomfortably, recalling that Christian T was stated as Flora's father.

"How terribly intriguing," chuckled Mickey, rubbing his beard.

"I'm going to be a student of his next term," declared Braden, "just wanted to know who I'll be dealing with."

Mickey directed them to a wooden bench across the road from the university.

"This is the most beautiful view in the village," he sighed waving his hand across the open countryside that sprawled into the distance, "it's a great place to think, have a few tipples and make out with a pretty girl," he snorted jovially.

Braden glanced towards Marley, who was stifling a giggle. Mickey was certainly full of character.

"So, the professor?" reminded Braden.

"Ahh yes! Very little is known about his family. It almost appears as though he doesn't have one, but then he is the heir to a small fortune and a disgustingly large estate, which must have been handed down by a relative. He carries the title of Lord, you know, though he seldom uses it."

"Lord...?" interrupted Marley apologetically.

"Hmmm let me think about that, it's an unusual name, not Irish for certain, almost sounds European," Mickey paused for a while, lost in thought, but the name didn't make an appearance, "I'll come back to that seems to be stuck in the recesses," he joked.

"What else can you tell me?" asked Braden.

"He likes to travel, never in the country for more than six weeks at a time. No one knows where he goes or what he's doing whilst he's away, but he's very well travelled."

"What about religion?" questioned Marley. "Do you know his denomination?"

Mickey frowned, the top of his forehead disappearing beneath a veil of grey hair as he did so.

"Now that's a difficult one. It's a subject he would never embark upon, almost shied away from religious topics outside of the lecture theatre, that is."

"Why do you think that was?" asked Braden.

"Not sure. It's one of those subjects that some people find taboo, although there was talk of him being an occultist."

Marley's ears pricked as she threw Braden a side glance, "like a devil worshipper?" she gleaned.

"I suppose of sorts, yes. You'll need to speak to Tabitha. She had a firsthand experience with him," replied Mickey.

"Oh, really, and where might we find Tabitha?" pleaded Marley.

"The public house, centre of the village, opposite the duck pond and cricket pitch. If you can hang on for five minutes, I'll take you there."

Mickey disappeared into the university, reappearing precisely five minutes later with his coat and hat.

The public house was quaint, desperately old, but cosy and welcoming. A hearty fire glowed in the hearth as they nestled beside it in soft leather chairs.

"Tabby!" shouted Mickey. "Got a minute?"

Tabitha was a robust woman with ample breasts and red hair.

"What can I do for you Mickey, my love?" she draped herself around Mickey's neck and began playing with his beard.

"Leave that for later," scolded Mickey, introducing Braden and Marley.

"Tell them about your encounter with professor T," demanded Mickey.

The woman's playful demeanour changed at the mention of the name.

"Why you dragging him up again? You know I don't like talking about him?" she pouted.

"My friends are curious honeybee, please," puckered Mickey, planting a wet kiss on her cheek.

Tabitha took a seat. She recalled the night she had been asked to attend a meeting in the basement of a big house.

"It was all a bit odd," she began, "I'd met this boy, my he was gorgeous, handsome, physically perfect, and I was happy to do anything if it meant getting his clothes off later!" Tabitha glanced at Mickey apologetically. "Sorry, love."

Mickey looked offended, but did his best to hide it behind a wry smile.

"Anyway," continued Tabitha, "we got into the basement. Weird writing on the walls and a group of people I didn't know swaying and humming rhythmically. In the centre of the group sat a man totally naked except for a long, hooded cloak. Eventually, the man stood up and held a large cup in the air. He drank from it and passed it around. When it got to my turn, I refused. How naïve did he think I was? The wine was probably drugged, and the man was hoping to have his wicked way with me. Not a chance, I was out of there without a second look back, but I couldn't find the exit," Tabitha stopped talking as she gulped, almost retching, "I'm sorry that's the way it makes me feel when I talk about it. Still gives me nightmares!"

"You managed to escape, though?" begged Marley.

"I did in the end, but not without a fight. The man caught hold of me, forced me to the floor, ripped at my clothing. I knew darn well what he was after, dirty old git. I scratched at his skin and threw back the hood, revealing none other than professor T, the latest member of the university teaching staff. I kicked him hard between the legs, he fell away from me. I raced through the crowd of astonished onlookers and found my way out through the entrance. I shudder to think what might have happened. Of course, I forfeited a night with the handsome boy I'd met and never saw him again, but at least I made it out with my chastity intact. Can you imagine…!"

Marley could imagine she was the one who didn't make it out. The one too naïve to refuse the chalice of wine. The one who suffered the consequences.

Braden touched her hand. He knew she was hurting.

"He left not long after that," added Mickey, "whether through shame or the fact that his secret pastime might be revealed to the village, one can only speculate."

"Shame!" scoffed Tabby. "The man didn't know the meaning of the word. Anyway, why you so interested in him? You a victim too?"

Her eyes met Marley's. The realisation was obvious. Both women had been victims at the hands of Professor T.

Tabby touched her hand. "You weren't quite so lucky, deary?"

Marley didn't need to answer, Tabby already knew.

XLVI

Sister Ophelia was feeling her way to freedom. She reached the brick wall of the fireplace and felt each brick, pushing forcefully, praying for one of them to be the key to her escape.

A muffled voice caught her attention. The professor was in his study. She stopped moving. Footsteps approached, followed by the scraping sound of brick grinding against stone.

Extinguishing the flame of candlelight, she shrank into the darkness, holding herself against the coolness of the stone wall. Daring not to move, not to breathe. She prayed for the shadows to camouflage her presence. She prayed for the professor to pass her by unnoticed.

She heard him enter, felt his presence and watched him for a fleeting moment as light from his study silhouetted his tall figure against the darkness.

She had to hurry if she were to make her exit. Once the professor realised she had escaped, he would come after her.

She hurled herself towards the fireplace, staggered to her feet, and hurried from the university without looking back. She felt the coolness of blood trickling down her legs; the book having oozed with blood as she'd landed with a thud upon the study floor.

She hurried towards the convent, holding it in her sight, longing for the security within its walls.

She was there now, closing the door behind her. She would be safe here, at least for the moment.

When Marley returned from Castle Craig, she headed for the convent. Sister Ophelia appeared at the door, nervous, shaking, and obviously distraught.

"What has happened, Sister?" demanded Marley.

The nun unburdened herself, recalling her capture at the hands of Edward Trent as Marley listened with a shocked expression.

"I'm certain he's the man I met on that fateful day almost eight years ago," added Marley, "and I'm certain he was sitting beside Braden on the bench, whether Braden remembers it or not."

Sister Ophelia agreed.

Marley then reported her date with Flora and the details of information gained on her trip to Castle Craig.

"I think something awful is about to happen, Sister," declared Marley. "I can feel it."

The nun nodded knowingly. "It is. The only consolation is that I retrieved the book."

She bustled Marley into her bedroom. Marley took one look at it and retched.

It reeked of evil.

"It's disgusting, I know, but it is the key to ending whatever Edward Trent has been planning for many years. Something that involves Flora," reminded the nun.

Marley's eyes widened at the sound of her daughter's name. She knew it was true, but how would the book help?

"Father Ignatius told me that everything I need to know to keep evil from destroying the world lies within the pages of this book, chapter 13, to be precise."

There was a glance between the two women. Marley stepped backwards as Sister Ophelia approached.

She made the sign of the cross upon its ugliness and dowsed it in holy water, then, holding her Bible and crucifix in one hand, she pulled back the cover of the book.

What happened in that moment and what the book revealed to her she cares never to reveal. She was plunged into the depths of hell. She witnessed the fall of humanity and the destruction of Christianity in one fleeting vision. Satan had conquered the earth.

"Sister, Sister!" Marley was shaking her back into consciousness.

The nun began to cry, an avalanche of tears cascading down her face. It was the empathy she felt for the world and its fate if she failed in her mission.

"Whatever did you see?" pleaded Marley.

The nun shook her head. "Something I cannot share, child."

The nun's bed was stained with blood, not bright in colour now or even recognisable in its consistency. This was almost black and thick, like tar. The book lay open, its pages unsullied, chapter 13 staring up at them.

"This is it, Marley," praised the nun as she gazed upon the chapter. "This is the depiction of the devil being slain. I must memorise its contents and pray for its deliverance. This is how we fight the greatest demon of all time... Satan!"

Marley feared the words that Sister Ophelia spoke. Slaying a demon. Was it even possible?

Sister Ophelia undressed and dropped to her knees. She read the book, then prayed all night and never stopped. It was only as dawn peered through her window that she rose to her feet.

Sister Grace knocked at the door and pushed it ajar. "Sister, are you all right? I missed you at breakfast."

Sister Ophelia hadn't realised the time. She hurried to the door.

"My goodness, what has happened to your hair?" shrieked Sister Grace.

The nun felt at the length of curls that flowed around her shoulders. It was only then that she caught sight of the colour. Her usually vibrant chestnut locks had turned deathly white.

XLVII

It was the day of Flora's eighth birthday and Mrs M. was scurrying around the house in a fluster.

She had hired the church hall for the afternoon, invited Flora's classmates, Marley, Sister Ophelia and, of course, Flora's foster family.

"Why are you in such a tizzy?" questioned Adam as he removed a third tray of buns from the oven.

"I just want it to be nice for Flora. This is probably the last time we shall all be together. She will be going to live permanently with her mammy and I doubt we will see much of her after that."

Adam kissed his mother's head tenderly.

"I'll take these round to the hall," he declared.

"Make sure your father has blown up all the balloons and that no one is eating the party food, especially Rory!"

Marley was waiting for Sister Ophelia to arrive. They were going to ride the bus to County Bottega together.

Braden was spending the afternoon watching cricket with Mr Brightman. The match hadn't started, but he'd settled in the lounge area with a bag of crisps and one of Mr Brightman's homemade beers.

"There's a gentleman on the telephone for you," announced Mrs Brightman, popping her head into the back parlour where the tv lived.

Braden knew the voice immediately as Mickey's voluminous tone sounded through the receiver.

"Mickey, to what do I owe the pleasure?"

"Just a quick call, old chap. I've suddenly remembered the professor's noble title."

Braden waited patiently as Mickey sidetracked with talk of the upcoming cricket game.

"The name Mickey!" he reminded.

"Sorry, yes it's... Lord Baloid."

"Baloid?" repeated Braden as Marley opened the front door to Sister Ophelia.

The name rang alarm bells with the nun. She was certain she had heard it or seen it somewhere before.

Braden smiled, "this is for the bus fare. Have a lovely time with Flora." He pushed a folded note into Marley's hand and patted her arm. "Now, if you'll excuse me, I think the crickets started."

A rain cloud followed their route to County Bottega, fine drops at first, which kept getting bigger and bigger until the full force of a thunderstorm threatened to greet them at their final stop.

A baby whimpered in its mother's arms, "apologies Sister," declared the woman as the nun turned towards her.

"No apology needed," replied Sister Ophelia. "May God bless your child."

"Thank you, Sister, she is being baptised next Sunday."

The nun smiled inwardly. New life was a blessing. Something she would have enjoyed had the Lord not called her to duty instead.

It was in that moment, as she gazed upon the innocent face of the child, that her memory returned.

She'd thought it odd at the time that a birth certificate should be so devoid of detail. The father had no surname except for the letter T, and the registrar's name was incomplete.

Sister Ophelia nudged Marley, who was busy taking in the view. "I know where I've heard that name."

"What name?"

"Baloid!"

Marley spun around, her expression questioning.

"Flora's birth certificate. The registrar's name is Baloid."

They continued the journey, contemplating the relevance of the unusual name and why it appeared on Flora's birth certificate.

The nun felt irritable as she bounced the name around in her thoughts. She was certain that Father Ignatius had also referred to it, though her recollection was vague. The events of the last couple of days were catching up with her. Perhaps the bump on the head didn't help. Her focus had to remain on the chapter of the book she had memorised. After all, it was the key to their very survival.

"Call this spring weather," moaned Marley as she and Sister Ophelia struggled against the force of wind and rain as they travelled the latter part of their journey on foot.

"This is nothing at the side of what we have yet to face," replied the nun with a grimace.

Marley chose not to think about that yet. It was her daughter's birthday and today was all about Flora.

They arrived at the birthday party drenched, their clothes, hair, and shoes dripping wet.

"Oh my," fussed Mrs M. "I don't know where this storm has come from. The weather channel certainly didn't forecast it."

"It's unpredictable like your mood swings, mother," declared Mr M with a smile and a cheeky wink.

Mrs M flushed as perspiration blotted her crisp white blouse. She was undergoing changes that women of her particular age experienced in midlife.

She shot her husband a disgruntled expression and wiped the moisture from her brow with the hem of a colourful apron.

"Where's the birthday girl?" asked Marley, excited.

Mrs M strained her neck and scoured the hall for Flora. Her eyes bounced from one child to the next, to the birthday cake standing proudly in one corner, and the neatly laid feast waiting to be unwrapped and ingested. Marley was not anywhere in sight.

"Odd! Let's try the toilets," declared Mrs M, bustling down the corridor, but the cubicles were empty.

A siren of panic pierced the air as Marley, Mrs M, and Sister Ophelia called out Flora's name.

"What's wrong mam?" questioned Adam, hearing the distressed tones.

"Have you seen Flora?"

Adam shook his head, "not for a while. She was talking to a well-dressed gentleman by the door."

"Someone we know?" demanded Mrs M.

Adam bowed his head.

"What have I said about strangers?" yelled Mrs M, throwing her hands into the air, "quickly run around to the vicarage and ask to use the telephone, says it's urgent."

"Who am I calling?" questioned Adam, unwittingly.

"The Police of course," screamed Mrs M.

Mr Moreton patrolled the perimeter of the church grounds. He drove around the community, stopping passersby to ask if they had noticed a pretty little girl and a well-dressed man together.

The police took descriptions, but that was about all they could do for the time being. They'd organise a search party if Flora didn't turn up in the next forty-eight hours.

"Mam!" the deep teenage tones of a prepubescent boy caught their attention.

"What is it Rory?" inquired a very irritated Mrs M.

"I found this." Rory handed over a half deflated yellow balloon. At first, its significance wasn't obvious, "there's writing on it."

TONIGHT, 8PM, YOU KNOW WHERE! emblazoned across it in thick, black letters.

"What does it mean?" urged Mrs M.

Marley and Sister Ophelia exchanged a knowing glance.

"I know where to find Flora," revealed the nun. "Do you think your husband would be so kind as to drive us home? Time is of the essence."

Within minutes Marley and the nun were racing down the narrow lanes of Ireland in the back seat of the Moretons car.

"Hold on," instructed Mr M as his foot hit the accelerator. He swung the old jalopy into action, mounting kerbs, almost hitting oncoming vehicles and barely avoiding a head on collision with a stray sheep.

Marley and the nun clung to each other as Mr M, in full racing driver mode, crunched his gears and exceeded the speed limit.

On an extremely sharp bend, he nudged a nearby tree trunk and ground to a halt.

Steam poured from beneath the bonnet of his beloved vehicle.

"Looks like the head gaskets blown," remarked Mr M from the depth of the car's engine.

"Can you fix it?" inquired Marley.

Mr M scratched his head, "afraid not, it's a job for an expert."

"How far from town are we?" added Sister Ophelia.

"A mile or two at most," he replied.

"We will have to journey on foot," advised the nun.

Marley agreed, "when we get to town we will send a mechanic out to you," she promised.

They left Mr M consoling himself, not just for the damage he had caused to his car, but for the expense he would face when fixing it and the wrath of Mrs M when she discovered his reckless behaviour.

It was almost six o'clock as they reached the B&B. The journey on foot had been fraught with danger. High-speed drivers, a herd of unruly cows and a cyclist who had almost knocked them down the hillside.

The storm that had followed them to County Bottega chased them home too, all the while gathering momentum. Bedraggled and soaked, they parted company.

"I'll meet you at the university gates just before eight," proffered Sister Ophelia as she sidled towards the convent in search of dry clothes.

Braden and Mr Brightman were asleep in front of the TV.

Marley woke him with a degree of urgency.

"Flora's been taken," she gasped anxiously.

"What? Where? By who?" he demanded.

"The university. The professor. We've got to go there tonight at 8," she revealed.

"You're soaking," observed Braden. "Go and change. I'll ask Mrs B to whip up some dinner for us. We're going to need our strength."

"We?" questioned Marley. "This isn't your fight, Braden. I can't ask you to put yourself in danger for me."

"You didn't ask, I offered," replied Braden, pulling her towards him and planting a delicate kiss on her lips.

Marley felt warmer already.

XLVIII

Sister Ophelia couldn't take her eyes off the grandfather clock that lived beside the front entrance of the convent. She watched the minutes ticking away with mounting anxiety.

"Sister... Sister... Sister!"

The nun was startled to find Sister Grace standing beside her. "Sorry, I was lost in thought," she revealed.

"Quite obviously. Have you heard that the new Mother Superior has been delayed yet again? Illness has thwarted her journey for another month."

"Really! That's nice," replied Sister Ophelia, who hadn't absorbed a word of Sister Grace's conversation.

"Are you all right?" begged Sister Grace, "I have seen little of you recently. You seem to spend more time away from the convent than you do in it."

"I've been busy Sister, there is just as much good to be done outside these walls as there is in them," replied the nun curtly.

Sister Grace crept away quietly.

Sister Ophelia headed towards Father Ignatius' old study. The room remained much as he had left it, unlike his bedroom, which had been packed away for his successor.

She sank into his chair beside the extinct fire. Fixed her gaze on the bureau that held his favourite tipples and sighed. No wonder the old priest had found solace at the bottom of a bottle, she thought. He must have faced constant trials of faith. Exorcism was not for the weak.

Tonight would test the foundation of her own belief. Tomorrow, if she survives, she may also look for comfort.

She bowed her head and prayed. In the moment's silence, she heard a thud; it caught her attention. A small book had fallen to the floor beside her feet. The nun looked around. Where did it come from? The nearest book shelf was on the other side of the room. She hadn't noticed it on the small table that partnered the old priest's chair, nor was it resting on the mantel of his fireplace.

It was a book of Bible verses belonging to the late Father Ignatius. The book lay open on a specific page, Thessalonians 3:3 "But the Lord is faithful, and He will strengthen and protect you from the evil one."

The nun smiled. "Thank you, father," she muttered as she digested the verse.

Marley and Braden were finishing dinner. The time had just passed seven thirty. Neither had really enjoyed their meal and were pushing it around the plate.

"Oh, I forgot to tell you," began Marley, breaking the cloud of silence that hovered between them, "Sister Ophelia remembered the name Baloid being written on Flora's birth certificate."

Braden looked confused. "Why would anyone write the professor's aristocratic title on a birth certificate, especially Flora's?"

"I think I know," added Marley, "I think your Professor T is the man who raped me. I think he is Flora's biological father."

Braden appeared shocked. "Are you certain?"

"As certain as I can be. I followed him, heard his voice. It was unmistakable."

Braden was lost in thought for a while, desperately trying to absorb the fact that his eminent professor could be capable of such atrocity.

"Got a pen?" he suddenly demanded.

Marley searched her bag without question.

Braden opened the tissue paper napkin that sat beside his plate and started writing.

"What are you doing?" queried Marley.

"I'm wondering whether those names are anagrams," he replied. "What was the name of the other guy who was there that night?"

"Christian T," she recited.

Marley wasn't sure of the meaning of anagram, but didn't want to appear foolish. She watched as Braden played with the letters, rearranging them into different orders.

"That's it," declared Braden, turning the napkin towards her.

Baloid had been changed to Diablo and Christian T to... Antichrist!

Marley couldn't believe her eyes. If this were true, then Flora's father was the Devil himself.

She felt nauseous, but there was no time for weakness. The clock had moved to ten before the hour. It was time for them to head to the university.

It was time for them to meet with the Devil!

XLIX

Sister Ophelia was waiting. Her face pale as she fumbled with her rosary uncharacteristically.

"You don't have to do this, neither of you," assured the nun. "This will be no ordinary battle and I hate to admit it, but we may not survive."

Marley turned to Braden. "I'm going in there to fight for my daughter. You have no reason to risk your life. Go back to the B&B, wait for me there. I can't have your unnecessary death on my conscience. There's been too much bloodshed already. Please Braden, let me do this on my own."

Braden realised the determination in Marley's eyes, and the nod of assurance from the nun.

"At least let me wait here for you. If you're both not out in an hour, I'm coming in."

Marley agreed. It seemed sensible to have someone on the outside, someone who could explain the events leading to their deaths if the need arose.

Braden planted a passionate kiss on Marley's lips. He turned to the nun, who stepped backwards.

"I was going to shake your hand, Sister," smiled Braden, "good luck and may your God be with you."

Sister Ophelia led the way to Edward Trent's study. The room stood empty, but the secretive brickwork that lead to the tunnel was ajar.

"Careful," warned the sister, "the floor is slippy and there's no light."

Marley followed as closely as she could. Her heart beat faster with every step forward.

It wasn't long before she caught the flicker of illumination in the distance.

"We're almost there," informed the nun. "Stay close to me. I have no idea what we are going to face."

Marley didn't need to be reminded. Memories of that night in the graveyard sprang into her thoughts. She attached herself to the back of Sister Ophelia as they stepped into the candlelight.

At first there was nothing to see except a circle of candles on a stone floor. Each standing at a distinctive point of the satanic pentagram.

"You came," declared a voice from the shadows. It was a voice both women recognised.

"You doubted I would?" replied the nun.

"I didn't think of you as such a risk taker, Sister. You survived last time, but I fear your luck may now have run out."

"Luck has nothing to do with it. My God will keep me safe, Professor. My faith will never betray me."

The figure of Edward Trent stepped into the light, a smirk crossing his lips. He wore nothing but a black robe, his bare flesh exposed on movement, and he carried a bronze cup in his right hand.

Marley gasped with fear. There stood the man she had met eight years ago, the man she had tried so hard to forget. The man who had ruined her life.

"I see you brought company," grinned Edward. "Step forward, my dear. Let me look upon you."

Marley moved cautiously, rubbing nervously at the silver crucifix hanging around her neck.

"Ahh yes, I remember you well," sneered the professor, "the taste of innocence, the purity of your form. How easily you gave yourself to me." He licked his lips erotically.

"Where's my daughter?" demanded Marley, the words trembling as she spoke.

"You do not have a daughter. The child you refer to is the direct descendant of Satan. You were merely the vessel that nurtured her."

"You are Satan, Lord Baloid?" queried Marley, feeling brave enough to ask.

There was a moment of hesitance as he devoured the unexpected declaration of his satanic name.

"I am many things and I have many names: Diablo, Devil, Antichrist, Lucifer. Take your pick."

"Give Flora back to us and we will keep your secret," begged Marley.

Edward Trent laughed maniacally, "you're bargaining with the Devil?"

Marley stepped forward, but Sister Ophelia held her back.

"That's right, Sister, protect your flock while you still have the chance," he mocked.

"I'm not afraid of you," declared the nun.

"Really? You should be!" growled the man, his voice deepening, "Flora, come child," he commanded.

The shadow of a small child stepped into view, still wearing her party dress and shoes. Outwardly, she looked like Flora, but it wasn't her. The beautiful blue of her eyes was black as night, lifeless and staring.

"Flora!" screamed Marley, almost knocking over a candle as she lurched towards her child.

"Do not enter the circle," warned the nun, holding her back. "That's what he wants you to do. His greatest power lives within it."

"You've done your homework Sister, I'm impressed," declared Edward, clapping his hands, "but nothing can save you now. Whether you step inside this circle or you don't, you're both going to die!"

Sister Ophelia stood firm. Her legs shook uncontrollably beneath her habit and her heart pounded like a hammer in her chest, but she could not reveal weakness to the demon before her.

"I think the least I deserve are answers," stated the nun unflinchingly.

"Ask away, Sister, my time is your time. For a few moments anyway."

"You used me to find Marley, tricked me. You made me think you wanted to help."

"Guilty!" groaned the man with a snigger.

"You raped a young woman!"

Edward glared, holding Marley in his gaze. He could no longer read her thoughts. He did not know the feelings that raged insider her, the volcano of hatred that bubbled beneath the surface.

"Eight years ago tonight, I conceived my offspring at 9 pm, and at the same hour, she will take over the world."

"You needed an heir!" observed the nun.

"You already have all the answers," he sneered.

"Not quite. What is the relevance of the eighth year?"

The professor stroked the child's hair before answering.

"It is the symbol of infinity, eternity, of endless possibilities. It is the age at which the child can assume responsibility."

His gaze turned upon the nun. "Have you finished playing for time now, Sister, with your insignificant questions?" he gloated.

"Did God forsake you, my son," demanded Sister Ophelia with determination, "were you abandoned, cast out of Heaven, thrown to the wolves?"

Edward grew angry. The candlelight that encompassed him burst into flame, jumping high into the air. His eyes glinting red beneath its glow.

"How dare you speak of your God," he hissed, flying towards them, passing untouched through the wall of fire, his voice grotesque, almost unrecognisable.

"There is only one true living God, who is infinite," quoted the nun.

Edward writhed, almost spilling the contents of his chalice.

"Drink and you shall live with your daughter for all time," he roared, offering the vessel to Marley, "drink as you did that night. A lamb to the slaughter, so easy to manipulate, so easy to control."

Marley stood frozen, held in the gaze of his piercing, hypnotic stare. For a moment, she felt the urge to accept. Her thoughts were awash with memories she'd tried so hard to forget. She felt the silver cross between her fingers and rubbed it. A reminder that she served only one God, and it wasn't Satan!

The nun breathed a sigh of relief as Marley turned away from him.

"I will save those who love me and will protect those who acknowledge me as Lord," recited Sister Ophelia.

Edward grew restless.

She repeated the words, this time louder and with conviction, holding forth her crucifix and showering him with holy water.

In his wrath, Edward had left the sanctity of the circle. He was vulnerable now. The holy water hissed as it touched his skin, frying the flesh beneath it.

Edward screamed, then placed the chalice to his lips and drank.

The air grew immediately colder as Edward twisted and writhed beneath the confines of his cloak. The evil that emerged from within was no longer human. Edward had transformed into the demon that disguised his true self, the demon known as Baloid.

"Sister!" shrieked Marley at the sight of his hideous form.

"Get behind me," demanded the nun, undeterred by the beast.

Marley didn't hesitate.

Sister Ophelia dangled her crucifix before the eyes of the beast and recited, "but the Lord is faithful. He will establish you and guard you against the evil one."

The beast groaned and pierced the air with an operatic scream.

"Reject every kind of evil," cried the nun, "be gone from this place Baloid, begone!"

Marley closed her eyes.

She felt the nun lurch forward, heard a blood-curdling howl, and then silence.

Hardly daring to open her eyes, she clung to the nun whose body quivered beneath her grasp.

Sister Ophelia sighed deeply.

"Is it over?" muttered Marley.

The nun did not reply. Her gaze firmly fixed upon the circle.

Marley moved forward. The demon had vanished.

"What happened?" she questioned, spying the empty bottle of holy water in the nun's hand.

"Shh," demanded the sister, "it isn't over, it's only just begun. The professor was a decoy!"

Marley gazed upon the circle of candles and screamed.

Flora was floating in the centre, black eyes wide, expression distorted, but she wasn't alone. Hovering beside her, his hand upon her shoulder was none other than Braden Finney.

Marley stuttered and stammered as the words she sought abandoned her.

Her newfound friend and her daughter. The questions were queueing for answers in her mind, but shock had kidnapped her speech.

Braden grinned.

"He is Satan!" announced Sister Ophelia.

"He can't be," denied Marley, suddenly finding her voice.

"As gullible as ever," remarked Braden, who was now standing before her.

"I don't understand…!"

"It's rather simple really, the professor was merely… How can I best describe him? My private investigator, my smoking mirror, my informant. I could go on, but frankly, I don't see the point."

Marley sank to the floor, her heart heavy with pain.

"It was all just an act, the pretence of caring for me, even helping me?" she challenged.

Braden threw up his hands.

"What can I say? You needed finding. Only with the child present can the prophecy be fulfilled," he smirked.

Marley felt wounded. She never could have imagined that the Braden she had grown close to was capable of such depravity and deceit.

"You don't recognise me, do you Marley?" he queried.

Marley shook her head and glanced towards Sister Ophelia.

"The eyes are the windows to the soul!" he sneered.

The nun had already solved the puzzle from the photograph of the young man in Flora's file. The secret lay within the eyes, as the demon had stated. The professor, Braden and Flora's father all viewed the world with the same eyes.

"He's Christian T," revealed the nun, "or rather the Antichrist."

Marley looked closer. There was a similarity now that she thought about it, the same distinctive stare. The one she had witnessed in Christian and Braden's eyes, but the face did not belong to Christian T. It was Braden's.

"Christian was executed right in front of me," she cried, "burned alive."

Braden sneered, "never heard of illusion? I haven't always lived inside this body, but when the professor told me he knew of your whereabouts, I needed to gain access to my child," he rubbed Flora's cheek roughly, "I remembered your penchant for charming young men."

Marley swelled with emotion. She wanted to swipe the condescending grin from his face. Every part of her wanted to scream, collapse to the floor and weep, but the nun needed her, her daughter needed her and, most of all, she wanted to destroy the entity that possessed Braden and deceived her.

Sister Ophelia could sense the power of the demon before her. The holy water had gone. All she had left was her crucifix, her faith, and the paragraphs she had memorised from chapter 13 of the Philosophy of Demons.

The Antichrist had forced the professor to reveal his identity and step outside the protective circle, at the precise moment that the nun's holy water sprayed across his body. It had been too easy to cast out Satan himself, she'd thought. She had been deceived and her defences weakened.

"You are Flora's biological father!" stated Marley.

The demon smirked, "I am Satan, and I have been controlling this child since the moment of conception," he announced with satisfaction.

Sister Ophelia cried out.

Satan adjusted his gaze.

"Of course I touched your life too, Sister, and that of your sibling and her child."

Marley grasped the nun's hand. She could see the pain in her expression, feel the loss she had endured.

Marley feared the Sister had lost hope. "God is standing beside us," she whispered, pushing an object into the nun's hand.

Sister Ophelia knew instantly what it was. She turned to Marley, who nodded reassuringly.

The nun clung to her crucifix once more and recited the Lord's prayer. Marley joined her.

Satan was not amused. He raised up his arms and cast the women aside. Marley hit the wall and dropped to the floor, only inches from the burning candles. Though heavily winded, she continued to pray.

Sister Ophelia collided with a wooden object, the lectern that had housed the Philosophy of Demons book. It had fallen apart on impact, spraying splinters across the floor, leaving two large pieces of wood lying on top of each other. She seized the opportunity and reached for the wood, crossing them in front of her, using the pieces as a large makeshift crucifix.

Marley blew at the candles closest to her. They extinguished, then lit again instantly.

Satan knelt before her, his eyes glowing crimson. He snarled like a wild animal as his forked tongue grew longer, writhing and curling from his open mouth, searching for Marley.

Sister Ophelia approached from the other side of the circle. She raised the makeshift cross as she continued to pray.

Satan turned his attention towards her.

"Your God can't save you, Sister," he hissed, as a hurricane of wind swept the nun off her feet, freeing her wimple as she wrestled against its strength, white curls curtaining her face. She raised her voice above the strength of its howl, desperate to be heard.

Marley grabbed a candle and hurled it towards the Devil. It missed him entirely and landed beside the nun.

Sister Ophelia looked at it, unscrewed the holy water in her hand, and doused the flame with a single drop. The glass bottle was the object Marley had placed there earlier.

Satan roared as the flame did not reignite. Marley threw another, and the same thing happened.

That was it. The candles were the key; they were protection; they kept the circle safe.

Marley crawled towards a third, but did not reach it before Satan tossed her into the air and held her there. This time, his forked tongue licked at her face as he drew her closer and closer to his ugliness.

Marley searched for the crucifix that hung around her neck. She yanked it from its position and drove it into the Devil's eye. He immediately dropped her as he fought with the holy object that obscured his vision.

Marley was half in the circle now. She reached the third candle and rolled it towards the nun.

Sister Ophelia was on her feet again. She doused the candle and moved towards her enemy.

She raised her rosary and bellowed, "begone, leave this place in the name of God the Father, God the Son and God the Holy Spirit."

For a brief moment, the Devil paused. Two candles remained on his pentagram. His strength had weakened, but he had a secret weapon, Flora.

He grabbed the child and pulled her towards him.

"Leave her alone," cried Marley.

The Devil sneered, "you would sacrifice yourself for your child?"

Marley, face covered in tears, nodded her head. "Yes, I would. Take me instead."

The Devil glanced upon the child, then thrust her aside.

He entwined himself around Marley until she was bound beneath his grasp. She retched beneath the tightness of his grip, almost vomiting from the stench of him.

Sister Ophelia couldn't break the prayer. She rushed forward and doused the remaining two candles with the last drops of holy water. Everything went black, only the flames in the Devil's eyes lit the darkness.

Satan screamed. Marley was released from his grip. She crawled towards Flora, who was lying face down on the stone floor.

Sister Ophelia faced the Devil with an air of contempt. If this were the moment that she died, then so be it, but she would do so fighting.

The Devil grabbed at her throat and squeezed. The nun gasped for breath as the pressure increased. This was it, she was sure of it. She was feeling drowsy, deprived of oxygen. Her eyelids felt heavy. She was losing consciousness.

Sister Ophelia felt herself floating away towards a bright light, though in the distance a woman's voice was calling her name. She could hear unbroken

Latin being spoken and Father Ignatius' voice whispering in her ear.

For a moment, there was silence. Her eyes flickered to life in the darkness. Marley was beside her, vigorously thumping at her chest.

"I'm okay," she mumbled, suddenly aware of her mortality.

Marley was hugging her now. "Oh Sister," she cried, "thank goodness."

For a moment, the nun didn't know if she was dead or dreaming. Everything was quiet, peaceful. Marley was safe, and Flora was standing beside her.

"How? What?" began the nun.

"Flora saved us," revealed Marley wiping at the tears that stained her face.

Sister Ophelia had witnessed none of it. She could only rely on Marley's recollection of events, though they were vague and disorganised.

Flora smiled through golden curls, her beautiful blue eyes glowing in the darkness.

"It's over," revealed the nun.

"You did it again," hugged Marley.

"No, we did it. If you hadn't brought that second bottle of holy water, I don't know how this would have ended and I don't care to think about it," praised Sister Ophelia.

Braden wasn't so lucky. The stranger he had met at the gates of the university that evening, whilst he waited for Marley to return, had possessed his body. He became a temporary host for Satan. His remains lay enclosed in the secret room behind the brick fireplace of the professor's study. Perhaps someone would discover him one day, perhaps not!

In the safety of the convent, Sister Ophelia buried Satan's book deep beneath the floor of the dungeon, as destroying it appeared to be impossible.

"I hope you forgive my weakness, Father Ignatius," despaired the nun, scolding herself for not having slain the demon herself. The professor's performance had caught her unaware. Thank God for Marley Sutton and her bottle of holy water.

Chapter 13 of the Devil's book had revealed that the candles were the key. Dowsing him with holy water made Satan vulnerable, but even then, she was no match for the power he exerted. Exorcism was definitely not her forte.

In the months that followed, Sister Ophelia prayed for direction. She eventually transferred to a mission overseas, where she hoped to make a difference. She could never forget the demons she encountered in Ireland. Their memories travelled with her no matter how many miles she put between herself and St Catharine's Convent.

Marley and Flora reunited. Mammy and daughter together again. Marley could start over, this time with Flora beside her. She would never forget the sacrifices made by those around her and she wept at Sister Ophelia's decision to leave the country, but at the end of the day, she was able to celebrate being mammy to a sweet, beautiful little girl.

After all, poor wee Flora was just an innocent child, a pawn immersed in an evil game over which she had no control...

Or did she?

Enjoyed reading Flora?

Review instantly!

It means a lot and goes a long way.

MORE FROM A G NUTTALL

DON'T WAKE THE MOON

Let The Darkness Sleep

The Meg Mysteries Series

WHEN THE RAVEN SINGS
WHEN THE TREES CRY
WHEN THE CURTAIN FALLS

Appreciations

A special thanks to my son, Oliver, without whom none of this would be possible.

Acknowledgements

Cover font(s)

[One of] The font used is Little Kids Handwriting. All rights are reserved by Cloudy's Fonts. Available at dafont.com.

Printed in Great Britain
by Amazon